11 $\frac{00}{n}$

THE PENOBSCOT MAN

RUNNING A LOG

THE
PENOBSCOT MAN

BY

FANNIE (HARDY) ECKSTORM

Short Story Index Reprint Series

BOOKS FOR LIBRARIES PRESS
FREEPORT, NEW YORK

First Published 1904

Reprinted 1970

INTERNATIONAL STANDARD BOOK NUMBER:
0-8369-3624-8

LIBRARY OF CONGRESS CATALOG CARD NUMBER:
74-128733

PRINTED IN THE UNITED STATES OF AMERICA

" For something about them, and the idea of them, smote my American heart, and I have never forgotten it, nor ever shall, as long as I live. In their flesh our natural passions ran tumultuous; but in their spirit sat hidden a true nobility, and often beneath its unexpected shining their figures took on heroic stature. — OWEN WISTER, *The Virginian*.

TO
John Ross
AND
The West Branch Drive

"That you and yours may know
From me and mine, how dear a debt
We owed you, and are owing yet
To you and yours, and still would owe."

CONTENTS

"And when I went to bid him welcome home, he told me that the history of your worship was already printed in books, under the title of 'Don Quixote de la Mancha;' and he says it mentions me too by my very name of Sancho Panza, and also the Lady Dulcinea del Toboso, and several other private matters which passed between us two only; insomuch that I crossed myself out of pure amazement, to think how the historian who wrote it should come to know them." — *The Adventures of Don Quixote de la Mancha,* Part II. book i. chap. 2.

INTRODUCTORY

THE question is sometimes asked why a state like Maine, so sparsely settled, poor, weak in all external aids, can send forth such throngs of masterful men, who, east and west, step to the front to lead, direct, and do. We who were brought up among pine-trees and granite know the secret of their success. It comes not wholly by taking thought: it is in the blood.

Here are stories of men, the kind we have yet a-plenty, who die unknown and unnoticed; and every tale is a true one, — not the chance report of strangers, the gleanings of recent acquaintance, the aftermath of hearsay, the enlargements of a fading tradition; but the tales of men who tended me in babyhood, who crooned to me old slumber-songs, who brought me gifts from the woods, who wrought me

little keepsakes, or amused my childish
hours, — stories which, having gathered
them from this one and that one who saw
the deed, I have bound into a garland to
lay upon their graves.

Such tales are numberless; choice be-
comes invidious unless rigidly limited, and
therefore, since the old West Branch Drive
is no more, I have chosen solely among
its members, and have strung these tales,
like beads of remembrance, upon one
thread, — of which we who love it never
tire, — the River.

These are stories told with little art. In
the long run, the books that lie closest to
the facts have the advantage. It is lovely
to be beautiful, but it is essential to be true.
The events are actual occurrences; the
names, real names; the places any one may
see at any time. Yet each story is not
merely personal and solitary, but illustrates
typically some trait of the whole class.
Their virtues are not magnified, their faults

are not denied; in black and white, for good or evil, they stand here as they lived, — as they themselves would prefer to stand on record. So they acted, thus they felt, these were their thoughts upon grave subjects: and it may be that the Penobscot man is a better, wiser, more serious man than even his contemporaries have judged him to be.

But one thing, from which we may glimpse the secret of the Maine man's success, cannot fail to impress whoever reads these tales, and that is that he dies so cheerfully. He is not concerned about himself, nor about his future in another world, so much as about his work here. For Death, he does not fear it. Sometimes he courts it, sometimes he scoffs it, sometimes he defies it; but always, always his work comes first. And however low it may seem, however crude, however inferior to that of the man of more culture, finer perception, larger opportunity, he likewise lives for an Ideal. For honor, for friendship, for emulation, for sport, for duty, for grim, stern, granite obstinacy, he risks his life and wills his will into achievement, or dies for his failure.

His morals — we will not speak of them ; his aspirations — *he* rarely talks of them ; his religion — well, Heaven send that there be many of us as sound in the righteousness of charity as he ! But his real strength is in his devotion to what he sets out to do. As Stevenson says of our late lamented Alan Breck : " Alan's morals were all tailfirst ; but he was ready to give his life for them, such as they were." And this is ever the litany of brave men the world over : A clear conscience, a good cause, O Lord, and, if it need me, the chance to die for it.

I

LUGGING BOAT ON SOWAD-NEHUNK

LUGGING BOAT ON SOWAD-NEHUNK

THIS is a Penobscot story.

When the camp-fire is lighted, and the smoke draws straight up without baffling, and the branches overhead move only as the rising current of heat fans them, then if the talk veers round to stories of crack watermen, and the guides, speaking more to each other than to you, declare that it was Big Sebattis Mitchell who first ran the falls at Sowadnehunk, — though full twenty years before, John Ross himself had put a boat over and come out right side up, — do not, while they are debating whose is the credit of being first, let slip your chance to hear a better tale : bid them go on and tell you how Joe Attien, who was Thoreau's guide, and his men who followed after and who failed, were the ones who made that day memorable.

And if your guides are Penobscot men, they will tell it as Penobscot men should, as if there were no merit in the deed beyond what any man might attain to, as if the least a man should do was to throw away his life on a reckless dare, and count it well spent when so lavished. For so are these men made, and as it was in those days of the beginning, so is it yet even to the present among us.

You will have heard, no doubt, of Sebattis, he who from his bulk was called by the whites Big Sebat, and from his lazy shrewdness was nicknamed by his tribesmen *Ahwassus*, the Bear. Huge and round he was, like the beast he was named for, but strong and wise, and in his dark, flat face and small, twinkling eyes there were resources, ambitions, schemes.

Scores of you who read this will recollect the place. In memory you will again pass down the West Branch in your canoe, past Ripogenus, past Ambajemackomas, past the Horse Race, into the welcome deadwater above Nesowadnehunk. There, waiting in expectancy for that glorious revelation of Katahdin which bursts upon you above Abol, that marvelous picture of the giant towering in majestic isolation, with its white "slide" ascending like a ladder to the heavens, you forgot yourself, did not hear the tumult of falling waters, did not see the smooth lip of the fall sucking down, were unconscious that just before you were the falls of Sowadnehunk. Then, where the river veers sharply to the right, you felt the guide spring on his paddle as he made the carry by a margin, and you realized what it would have been to drift unguided over those falls.

So it has always been, — the sharp bend of the river to the right, blue, smooth, dazzling ; the carry at the left, bare, broad, yellow-earthed. Crossing it forty rods, you cut off the river again, and see above you to the right the straight fall, both upper and lower pitches almost as sheer as mill-dams, and in front the angry boil of a swift current among great and thickset rocks. So it always stays in memory, — at one end the blue river, smooth and placid, and the yellow carry ; at the other, the white hubbub of tossing rapids below perpendicular falls.

One May day long ago, two boats' crews came down to the carry and lugged across. They had lugged three miles on Ripogenus, and a half mile on Ambajemackomas, besides the shorter carry past Chesuncook Dam; they had begun to know what lugging a boat meant. The day was hot, — no breeze, no shade; it was getting along toward noon, and they had turned out, as usual, at three in the morning. They were tired, — tired, faint, hot; weary with the fatigue that stiffens the back and makes the feet hang heavy; weary, too, with the monotony of weeks of dangerous toil without a single day of rest, the weariness that gets upon the brain and makes the eyes go blurry; weary because they were just where they were, and that old river would keep flowing on to Doomsday, always drowning men and making them chafe their shoulders lugging heavy boats. There was not a man of them who could not show upon his shoulder a great red spot where the pole used in lugging boat, or the end of an oar on which barrels of pork or flour had been slung in carrying wangan, had bruised and abraded it. And now it was more lugging, and ahead were Abol and Pockwockamus and Debsconeag and Passangamet and Ambajejus and Fowler's and — there are, indeed, how many of them! The over-weary always add to present burdens that mountain of future toil.

So it was in silence that they took out the oars and seats, the paddles and peavies and pickaroons, drew the boats up and drained them of all water, then, resting a moment, straightened their backs, rubbed the sore shoulders that so soon must take up the burden again, and ran their fingers through their damp hair. One or two swore a little as relieving their minds, and when they bent to lift the boat, one spoke for all the others.

" By jinkey-boy! " said he, creating a new and fantastic oath, " but I do believe I'd rather be in hell to-day, with ninety devils around me, than sole-carting on this carry."

That was the way they all felt. It is mighty weary business to lug on carries.

For a driving-boat is a heavy lady to carry.
The great Maynards, wet, weigh eight to
nine hundred pounds, and they put on
twelve men, a double crew, to carry one.
The old two-streakers (that is, boats with
two boards to a side where the big Maynards had three) were not nearly so heavy,
and on short carries like Sowadnehunk
were lugged by their own crews, whether
of four men or six; but diminishing the
crew left each man with as great a burden.
A short man at the bow, another at the
stern, with the taller ones amidships under
the curve of the gunwale if they were lugging without poles, or by twos fore, aft,
and amidships for six men lugging with
poles, was the usual way they carried their
boats; and it was "Steady, boys, steady;
now hoist her!"—"Easy, now, easy; hold
hard!" for going downhill she overrode
John and Jim at the bow, and going up
a rise Jack and Joe at the stern felt her
crushing their shoulders, and when the
ground was uneven with rocks and cradle-
knolls, and she reeled and sagged, then
the men at the sides caught the whole

weight on one or the other of them. Nothing on the drive speaks so eloquently of
hard work as the purple, sweat-stained cross
on the backs of the men's red shirts, where
the suspenders have made their mark; they
get this in lugging boat on carries.

But they bent their backs to it, wrig-
gled the boat up and forward to her place,
each crew its own boat, and staggered on,
feet bracing out, and spike-soled shoes
ploughing the dirt and scratching on the
rocks. They looked like huge hundred-
leggers, Brobdingnagian insects, that were
crawling over that yellow carry with all
their legs clawing uncertainly and bracing
for a foothold. The head boat crowded
Bill Halpin upon a rock so hard that he fell
and barked his shins on the granite ; that
dropped the weight suddenly upon Jerry
Durgan's shoulder, so that a good two
inches of skin was rasped off clean where
it had been blistered before; little Tomah
Soc stumbled in a hole, and not letting go
his grip, threw up the other gunwale so that
it half broke his partner's jaw. Those boats
took all the mean revenges wherewith a

driving-boat on land settles scores for the rough treatment it receives in the water.

They were lugging that May morning only because no boat could run those falls with any reasonable expectation of coming out right side up. For up to that time they had chiefly used the Wallace boat, built low and straight in the gunwale, raking only moderately at the bow and low in the side. It is related that when the great high-bowed Maynard batteaus were first put on the river, short old Jack Mann, who was pensioned in his latter days by P. L. D.,[1] looked with high disfavor on the big, handsome craft, and then, rushing into the boat-shop, demanded an axe, an auger, and a handsaw.

" What 's that for ? " asked the foreman, suspecting that it was but one of Jack's devices for unburdening his mind in some memorable saying.

[1] The Penobscot Log-Driving Association, known as P. L. D. to distinguish it from P. L. A., the Penobscot Lumbering Association. It is always called either "P. L. D." or "The Company." It owns all dams, booms, etc., and annually sells the drive at auction to the bidder contracting to take the logs down at the lowest rate per thousand.

"Want 'em to cut armholes in that blasted boat," growled Jack, insinuating that the bows were above the head of a short man like himself.

But the old boat,— you may yet sometimes see the bones of one of them bleaching about the shores of inland ponds, or lying sun-cracked in the back yards of country farms, — stable and serviceable as she was, was no match for this handsome lady of to-day. They run the Arches of Ripogenus now with all their boats, and have done it for years ; but at the time when Sebattis came down to Sowadnehunk, such water no man ever dreamed of running. It is likely enough that Sebattis, just back from a sixteen years' residence at Quoddy, did not know that it had ever been run successfully.

Be that as it may, when Sebattis and his bowman came down, the last of three boats, and held their batteau at the taking-out place a moment before they dragged her out and stripped her ready to lug, what Sebattis, as he sat in the stern with his paddle across his knees, said in In-

dian to his bowman was simply revolu-
tionary.

"Huh?" grunted his dark-faced partner, turning in great surprise; "you
t'ought you wanted run it dose e'er falls?
Blenty rabbidge water dose e'er falls!"

The bowman had stated the case con-
servatively. That carry was there merely
because men were not expected to run
those falls and come out alive.

But the bowman's objection was not
meant as a refusal: he knew Sebattis, that
he was a good waterman, few better. A
big, slow man, of tremendous momentum
when once in motion, it was likely enough
that all the years of his exile at Quoddy he
had been planning just how he could run
those falls, and if he spoke now, it was
because this was the hour striking. In his
own mind he had already performed the
feat, and was receiving the congratulations
of the crowd. It was no small advantage
that he knew an audience of two boats'
crews was waiting at the lower carry-end to
testify, however grudgingly, to the authen-
ticity of what he claimed to have done.

The bowman had faith in Sebattis ; as he listened to the smooth stream of soft-cadenced Indian that cast silvery bonds about his reluctance and left him helpless to refuse (Sebattis being both an orator in a public and a powerful pleader in a private cause), the bowman caught the rhythm of the deed. It was all so easy to take their boat out into midstream, where the current favored them a little, to shoot her bow far out over the fall, and, as the crews ashore gaped in horrified amazement, to make her leap clear, as a horse leaps a hurdle. And then to fight their way through the smother of the whirlpool below, man against water, but such men as not every boat can put in bow and stern, such strong arms as do not hold every paddle, such great heads for management, such skill in water-craft as few attain.

This was the oration, with its Indian appeal to personal glory. It was, as Sebattis said, " *Beeg t'ing*," and he fired his bowman with the desire for glory. The Penobscot man, white man or Indian, dies with astonishing alacrity when he sees anything worth dying for. And the name of "crack waterman" is a shining mark to strive for.

Thus at the upper end of the carry Sebattis·and his bowman talked over at their leisure the chances of dying within five minutes. At the other end the two boats' crews lay among the blueberry bushes in the shade of shivering birch saplings and waited for Sebattis. It did not worry them that he was long in coming; they knew the leisurely Indian ways, and how unwilling, though he weighed hard upon two hundred and sixty, and had strength to correspond, was Big Sebattis to lug an extra pound. They pictured him draining his boat and sopping out with a swab of bracken the last dispensable ounce of water, then tilting her to the sun for a few minutes to steam out a trifle more before he whooped to them to come across and help him. It did not worry them to wait, — it was all one in the end: there would be carries to lug on long after they were dead and gone.

So, looking at the logs ricked up along the shores and cross-piled on the ledges, looking at the others drifting past, wallowing and thrashing in the wicked boil below the falls, they lounged and chaffed one another. Jerry Durgan was surreptitiously laying cool birch leaves on his abraded shoulder, and Bill Halpin was attentively, though silently, regarding his shins : there had been none too much stocking between him and that " big gray." The Indians, stretched out on their backs, gazed at the sky ; nothing fretted them much. On one side, an Indian and an Irishman were having a passage at wit ; on the other, two or three were arguing the ins and outs of a big fight up at 'Suncook the winter before, and a Province man was colloguing with a Yankee on points of scriptural interpretation. It was such talk as might be overheard almost any time on the drive when men are resting at their ease.

"It was French Joe that nailed Billy ; Billy he told me so," came from the group under the birches.

From among the Indians out in the sunlight arose a persuasive Irish voice.

"Why is it, Tomah, that when your folks are good Catholics, and our folks are good Catholics, you don't ever name your children Patrick and Bridget?"

And the reply came quick : " 'Cause we hate it Irish so bad, you know!"

Off at the right they were wrangling about the construction of the Ark.

" And I 'd just like to have seen that bo't when they got her done," said the Yankee; "just one door an' one winder, an' vent'lated like Harvey Doane's scho'l'ouse. They caught him nailin' of the winders down. ' How be ye goin' to vent'late?' says they. ' Oh,' says he, 'fresh air 's powerful circulatin' stuff; I callate they 'll carry the old air out in their pockets, an' bring in enough fresh air in their caps to keep 'em goin';' an' that was all they ever did get 's long 's he was school agent. My scissors! three stories an' all full of live-stock, an' only one winder, an' that all battened down! Tell you what! I 'd 'a' hated to be Mr. Noah's fambly an' had to stay in that ole Ark ten months an' a half before they took the cover off! Fact! I read it all up onct!"

Said another: " I don't seem to' member

how she was built, 'ceptin' the way they run her seams. She must have ben a jim-dickey house with the pitch all on the inside's well as on the outside o' her. Seems to me a bo't ain't bettered none by a daub o' pitch where the' ain't none needed."

" 'T ain't the Ark as bothers me some," put in the Province man ; " I reckon that flood business is pretty nigh straight, but I could n't never cipher out about that Tower of Babel thing. Man ask for a hod o' mortar, an' like enough they'd send him up a barrel of gaspereau ; that's " —

The religious discussion broke off abruptly.

" Holy   Hell ! — Look   a-comin' ! " gasped the Yankee.

Man ! but that was a sight to see ! They got up and devoured it with their eyes.

On the verge of the fall hovered the batteau about to leap. Big Sebat and his bowman crouched to help her, like a rider lifting his horse to a leap. And their eyes were set with fierce excitement, their hands cleaved to their paddle handles, they felt the thrill that ran through the boat as they shot her clear, and, flying out beyond the curtain of the fall, they landed her in the yeasty rapids below.

Both on their feet then! And how they bent their paddles and whipped them from side to side, as it was "In!"—"Out!" —"Right!"—"Left!" to avoid the logs caught on the ledges and the great rocks that lay beneath the boils and snapped at them with their ugly fangs as they went flying past. The spray was on them; the surges crested over their gunwales; they sheered from the rock, but cut the wave that covered it and carried it inboard. And always it was "Right!"—"Left!"— "In!"—"Out!" as the greater danger drove them to seek the less.

But finally they ran her out through the tail of the boil, and fetched her ashore in a cove below the carry-end, out of sight of the men. She was full of water, barely afloat.

Would Sebattis own to the boys who were hurrying down through the bushes that he had escaped with his life only by the greatest luck? Not Sebattis!

"Now you bale her out paddles," said he to his bowman, and they swept her with their paddles as one might with a broom.

"Now you drain her out," commanded Sebattis, when they could lift the remaining weight, and they raised the bow and let the water run out over the slanting stern, all but a few pailfuls. "Better you let dat stay," said the shrewd Sebattis.

It was quick work, but when the crew broke through the bushes, there stood Sebattis and his bowman leaning on their paddles like bronze caryatids, one on either side of the boat. They might have been standing thus since the days of the Pharaohs, they were so at ease.

"Well, boys, how did you make it?" queried the first to arrive on the spot.

Sebattis smiled his simple, vacuous smile. "Oh, ver' good; she took in lill' water mebbe."

"By gee, that ain't much water! Did she strike anything?"

Sebattis helped to turn her over. She had not a scratch upon her.

Then the men all looked again at the

boat that had been over Sowadnehunk, and they all trooped back to the carry-end without saying much, two full batteau crews and Sebattis and his bowman. They did not talk. No man would have gained anything new by exchanging thoughts with his neighbor.

And when they came to the two boats drying in the sun, they looked one another in the eyes again. It was a foregone con-clusion. Without a word they put their galled shoulders under the gunwales, lifted the heavy batteaus to their places, and started back across that carry forty rods to the end they had just come from.

What for? It was that in his own esteem a Penobscot man will not stand second to any other man. They would not have it said that Sebattis Mitchell was the only man of them who had tried to run Sowad-nehunk Falls.

So they put in again, six men to a boat, full crews, and in the stern of one stood Joe Attien, who was Thoreau's guide, and in the bow Steve Stanislaus, his cousin. That sets the date, — that it was back in

1870,—for it became the occasion for another and a sadder tale. If only Steve Stanislaus had held that place for the rest of the drive, it is little likely that we should have to tell the story of the death of Thoreau's guide.

And they pushed out with their two boats and ran the falls.

But the luck that bore Sebattis safely through was not theirs. Both boats were swamped, battered on the rocks into kindling wood. Twelve men were thrown into the water, and pounded and swashed about among logs and rocks. Some by swimming, some by the aid of Sebattis and his boat, eleven of them got ashore, "a little damp," as no doubt the least exaggerative of them were willing to admit. The unlucky twelfth man they picked up later, quite undeniably drowned. And the boats were irretrievably smashed. Indeed, that was the part of the tale that rankled with Sebattis when he used to tell it.

"Berry much she blame it us" (that is, himself) "that time John Loss." (Always to the Indian mind John Ross, the head contractor of the drive, was the power that commanded wind, logs, and weather.) "She don' care so much 'cause drowned it man, 'cause she can get blenty of it men; but dose e'er boats she talk 'bout berry hard."

That is how they look at such little deeds themselves. The man who led off gets the credit and the blame; he is the only one remembered. But to an outsider, what wins more than passing admiration is not the one man who succeeded, but the many who followed after and failed, who could not let well enough alone when there was a possible better to be achieved, but, on the welcome end of the carry, the end where all their troubles of galls and bruises and heavy burdens in the heat are over, pick up their boats without a word, not one man of them falling out, and lug them back a weary forty rods to fight another round with Death sooner than own themselves outdone.

II

THE GRIM TALE OF LARRY CONNORS

THE GRIM TALE OF LARRY CONNORS

It is hardly conceivable that at noon of a hot summer day, in clear sight and clear sunshine, not a cloud nor a shadow to suggest a mystery, a keen, shrewd, practical business man, one of the head contractors of a big concern like the West Branch Drive, should think he saw a ghost, more especially when the apparition was topped by a flaming hat of scarlet felt and accompanied by two manifestly flesh-and-blood woodsmen not unknown to him. But so it fell out at the Dry Way of Ripogenus. And "Jim" owned up to his scare.

"By gum," said he, when he met me afterwards, "but you had me that time." And there would have been no sense in denying it, for he had given a snort like a startled buck, and even at ten rods away his attitude of surprise and consternation betrayed him. "Seeing you come up out of that hole with that red hat on, I thought for sure you must be the ghost of Larry Connors. I 'd passed there not half a minute before, and not seen nothin', the bank 's so steep there. Then I looked back over my shoulder and up pops that red hat; thought for a secont that the everlastin' ha'nts had got me sure!"

Years afterward I was talking with a riverman of the old school. "And have you been up *there!* And *do* you know the Big Heater, and the Little Heater, and the Big Arches, and the Little Arches! And say, now, do you *know* about Larry Connors! Well, I want t' know, you *do* know all about Larry Connors! Smartest man ever was on the West Branch Drive!" And then the rosy sunset of his recollection burned away to ashen thoughts. "But they never found nothin' of him," he said slowly and sombrely.

"Lewey Ketchum" — said I.

"Yes — Lewey Ketchum — that 's so — down to the Big Eddy," said he, and stopped. It was plain he knew the story.

But this was long since, by virtue of being taken in broad daylight for the ghost of Larry Connors, I came into possession of the facts about his death. One and another told it, each one adding something; bit by bit I patched the whole together till I made the story out.

"Yes, old Jim he got his hoops started all right enough;" said one of the men. "He would n't ha' owned up to it, if there had been any other way out. You see, Larry was killed right about that very spot. And the drive had all gone along, and Jim he 'd just come down, — had n't even heerd of your bein' here, — an' most like 's he was just sa'nterin' along the drivin'-path, not expectin' to see no one, he got to thinkin' about Larry. Then he seen your red hat, and that fixed him. You see, Larry alwers wore somethin' red on his head; that red topknot was his trade-mark; did n't seem to make much differ what it was, a cap, or a handkerchief, or a red band round his hat, or the end of an old comforter pulled on, — just as far as you could see him, there would be

Larry's red comb sticking up, and him just whelting into the logs and swearin' to beat seven of a kind. There's no mistakin' but Larry was a turrible able man."

But what was there about Larry Connors that, so many years after his death, could conjure up his ghost in broad day, bright sunlight, open spaces, to affright a sober, shrewd, hard-headed business man? Not, certainly, that he wore a fantastic headdress and died in the Dry Way of Ripogenus. Many are the men that have gone down in the morning to work on the logs in that gorge, men of blood and bone, who at evening, as thin, impalpable ghosts, have stolen up from Ripogenus to whatever land of shades and twilight duskiness — growing, let us hope, to brighter dawning — is allotted to men, not righteous, nor moral, nor admirable altogether, but yet dying ungrudgingly for their work. Throngs of such have traveled up the gorge of Ripogenus since Larry Connors died there thirty years ago, and yet of them all you will hear no name so often repeated, no story so many times rehearsed, as the grim tale of Larry's going. Somehow the men do not seem to forget Larry Connors. He stands for somewhat more than fantastic headgear and spectacular annihilation.

Larry Connors was an Exchange Street Irishman, and the best of his education he acquired upon the logs at City Point. By the time he was graduated from the supervision of the truant officer, he was capable of doing anything on logs. He was utterly fearless, thoroughly efficient, a fighting Irishman of the old bulldog type, close-haired, crop-eared, bullet-headed, ready always to show his teeth — less only the front one knocked out in a fight — with reason or without. Yet the men liked him. My father, for whom he worked all one winter in the woods, always had a good word for Larry, that he was a hard worker, a quiet man in camp, and — which is perhaps the most remarkable thing ever said of Larry Connors — that he never heard him swear.

This commendation must stand unique. For I have heard it said by one of his mates that Larry was "the wickedest man that ever went on the West Branch Drive."

"And you had n't better not believe," my informant went on, sowing his negatives with so lavish a hand that it was doubtful whether the crop would grow up odd or even, "you had n't better not believe that this West Branch Drive ain't not no holy Sunday-school!" Being bred up to the Maine woods and its speech, I understood him to imply that Larry was notoriously profane; that was certainly his meaning. Yet had Larry killed a man, or been of vicious and irreclaimable temper, or of bestial cruelty, or implacable in revenge, — even then, though he might have been avoided as a "bad" man, he would hardly have been condemned as a "wicked" one. No, the wicked man is the profane swearer, the unprovoked blasphemer.

How does it happen, inquires the stranger, that in a country where neither dog, horse, ox, nor log will move till it is prodded with an oath, where profanity is general rather than the exception, and there is a variety and ingenuity and artistic finish

about even the commonplace cursing that
marks it as the work of no unpracticed
tongue, how does it happen that this com-
monest vice of all is selected as the most
censurable?

In its common forms it is neither cen-
sured nor censurable especially, nor is it a
vice; it is a vulgarity. There is no harm
intended by the pleasant maledictions of
every-day life, the oath of emphasis, the
oath of affection, the oath of good-fellow-
ship just to make you feel at home, the
picturesque and kindly cursing of the fellow of scanty vocabulary. But now and
then arises a man of different temper, who
blasphemes violently, who studies it as an
art, who, not using it as a neighborly by-
path of speech, so lavishes his energies on
purely rhetorical anathemas that he chills
the blood of even these seasoned woodsmen and rivermen. Such men, they say,
will sometimes swear five minutes at a time
without stopping, and swear "most hor-
rid;" and these they say are "wicked men,"
because, as they know from dread experi-
ence, no man can thus defy the Almighty

and come out scathless. Hence the over-powering impiousness of those like Larry Connors, upon whom the judgment was swift and sure. This is why the man is still remembered.

Yet if you dare assume that it was not a judgment, no man agrees with you. There were enough that day who heard him say that he would break that jam or go to hell doing it. How many of those who have spoken to me have spoken as eye-witnesses! "I was right there!"— "I should have been with him on the logs, but I had just gone ashore for my axe."—"I saw the whole thing."—"I did n't see it, but I could hear it all, and the man next to me he said, 'There 's some poor fellow gone; guess it must be Larry.'"—"Yes, he did say just them very words, for I was right by and heard it." One after another, though it is thirty years since and the ranks are thinning, has rehearsed the scene and his words. For they all know how Larry Connors died at the Dry Way of Ripogenus.

In those days the Dry Way was not a

dry way, but a waterway. They have tamed the River since then, and this is one of the places where it wears the curb. Rough as it is to-day, the River is a chained beast beside what it once was. To-day, where channels divide, wing-dams throw all the water into one thoroughfare; to-day there is a great dam at the head of Ripogenus Gorge, with gates to control the water and the sluicing; to-day, by night and by light, men stand on every commanding point, waving a firebrand if it is dark, their hands by day (unless already the telephone has superseded these), watching and signaling if the logs catch on; in two minutes word goes up from the Little Arches three miles below, and the sluicing stops till the jam is cleared. No longer do the great sticks come leaping up on the backs of those already stranded, uncounted and uncontrollable. And to-day, if a jam does form, there is a little shed by the dam where dynamite is kept; enough of that will remove the stubbornest obstruction. But the older men will tell you how in their youth, that is, in Larry Connors' day, they were let down by ropes from the cliffs at the Big Heater, to hang like dangling spiders from a thread when the jam broke under them; how they watched and warred on the Arches; how they held the perilous pass by the Little Heater against leaping timbers; how they fought for life with the wild logs below the Dry Way. In Larry Connors' day it was "We who are about to *die*, salute you." They died, — they never surrendered, — that is why the River has been conquered.

There is three miles of this turbulent water, the roughest that the will of man ever brought to heel and made to carry his freights for him. Those who have seen it in the drought of August, when the lakes are emptied and the current is weak and lagging, have no conception of the grandeur of the spring torrent. "Three miles of Niagara," a lumberman once called it, and the phrase well describes this canyon, ripped out of the solid rock, with sheer and often inaccessible walls, and the rock-ribbed, boulder-studded river-bed, falling more than seventy feet to the mile, down which rushes a boiling, seething, smoking flood of water, all a-lather in its haste.

The worst place upon it is just at the head of the gorge as the waters leave the lake. Here an island divides the channel, and a great dam is stretched across both branches of the river. The part of the dam on the north is pierced for sluice and gate ways; the southern portion is a side-dam, without gates, to cut the water off entirely from the lesser channel. Down one side of the island race the white horses of the falls, tossing their manes, thundering, smashing, flying in a smother of foam as they press through the Gorge of the Perpetual Rainbow. Down the other side lies the Dry Way, and here the former riverbed is scraped to the bone, bare of all water but a silvery trickle, with beetling sides of bare and shining rock. What a contrast between this and the waterway the other side of the island! There they never attempt to clear a jam; they let it catch and grow, and soon the pressure of the water behind it tears all away, snapping the largest logs like willow wands, tossing them thirty feet in air. " We never put a man on there to clear a jam," Joe Francis told me, and he was boss of the whole drive that year; "we let it form and pile up, and the water tears it all away." Nor would he even let us go to look at it until they were done sluicing, on account of the danger from leaping logs.

Once, before the dam was built, the Dry Way was like that, too. In Larry Connors' day, it was not dry but a waterway like the other. It was just here by the foot of the island, where the southern shore sweeps round like an amphitheatre, that a jam had formed that day when Larry made his last bid against death, for the glory of being looked at.

It was not a big jam, only a hundred and fifty or two hundred thousand feet of pine; but it was a bad one, held by a single key-log. The boss of that crew had been on it and sounded it. He had come ashore with his hand on his chin. He was a Spencer, and if any one knows logs and water it ought to be a Spencer, — Veazie, or Oldtown, or Argyle, they are all rivermen. Thirteen springs this one worked on the West Branch Drive, and it rested with him to say what was to be done now.

"What d' ye think of it, Steve?" asked one of the men.

"Think?—I think it is a devil of a jam for a little one," said he; "I'm still thinking."

An old riverman had undertaken to tell the tale, and he went on:—

"Course the fellows was all hangin' round waiting to be ordered on. They had their peavies with them, and was just a-holdin' for the word how to take it.

"'It's all right for a jam,' said Steve; 'when she hauls, she'll go clearn to thunder, and it won't cost the Comp'ny a red for pickin' up the pieces; whole thing hangs on one key-log, 's neat and pretty as a basket of chips, and jest about as safe as a berrill of gunpowder on the Fourth o' July; when she goes, she'll go tearin'. Sorry to disapp'int ye, boys, but I guess I won't drownd any of ye to-day. We'll dog-warp this off. Get the tackle and take a hitch around that key-log, and we'll put on men enough to send her flukin'.'

" Well, boss is boss, and boss is s'posed to have things his own way ; but there was boys there that would n't listen to this. Safe ways o' doin' things wa'n't what they was cryin' for. Out steps Larry, and he did look the able man for sure, calked shoes and a blue shirt, his trousers cut off at the knees and more rags 'n patches. And he had a red handkerchief tied round his head kind o' cocky, so the tails of it flew out. He just swung his peavey up on his shoulder and planted hisself, with one hand held out — well, they don't make abler men to look at.

" ' Look a-here, Steve,' says he, ' I 'm beggin' the chance.'

" ' I know you are a crack man, Larry,' says Steve ; ' but I 'd ruther drownd a poorer one; mine 's the best way, Larry,' says he, kind o' coaxin' him.

" Then Larry turns round to the boys, and sorter smiled at 'em. It was the big dare he was givin' 'em, but he did n't speak it loud, only smilin' like 's if he thought they was an easy crew to beat out.

" It 's my job, boys,' says he, sort o' satisfied ; ' I 'll go a step beyond any man in *this* crew.'

"And he had n't not got the words out'n his mouth when out steps Charley Rollins of Veazie, and Rollins says, says he : ' The man that goes a step ahead of me he goes to hell ! ' says he.

" Well, that fixed it. Larry sprung his knees a little 's if to limber 'em, an' he says, ' That's all right, Charley ; that's a bully bluff, but I 'll raise you.'

" There would n't have been any holding them back after that. Them two was in the same bo't together, and they 'd been runnin' races all the spring to see which could get into the most bad places. No matter who else had volunteered, after that it was betwixt them two to cut that key-log.

" So the rest of the crew took their pea-vies, and they got their axes, and they all went out on the logs. I s'pose it was long 'bout here that Larry went back to camp and got a luncheon, because it was Rollins's turn to go first. Anyway, Larry goes up to camp, and he sets down under the bushes and commences to fire bits of waste

biscuit at a squirrel that was around fillin'
up his wangan on sody bread, an' says he,
'Say, cooky,'—Furbish was cook that
year, he told us all what Larry said arterwards,—'say, cooky, gimme a hatful o'
biscuit an' a hunk o' hoss; I 'm hungrier
'n an owl on Friday. Just ben down to
the foot o' the Island, an' they 've got the '
—well, he said they had the—the—
donno 's I can justly remember what it
was that he *did* say." There was a bland
ingenuousness about the evasion which I
admired as coming from one whose pho-
nographic memory was never known to
blur a record. "But he told cook, says
he, ' I 'm goin' to break that jam, if I go
to hell doing it.' Them 's just his words;
mebbe he said more arterwards, I don't
know, Larry was quite a hand to talk, he
did n't know no better; but he did say
that he would break that jam or go to
hell doing it, all the boys testified to that.

"Well, it was Rollins's turn to go on
first, as I was sayin'. You see, in a bad
place they spell men; that 's the custom.
It don't do to have a man git all tuckered

out with hard work and then have to run for his life when he hain't nother lungs nor limbs to help him; for the minit she cracks he's got to jump and run like thunder. So when the boss thinks that the first one's done all that's good for him, he calls him back and sends out another man. O' course the last one has the wust chance. Now Larry made the dare, and he was the one that raised it, and it was his right to get in the last clip at that log — that's what he was biddin' for. And that's why Rollins went on first.

"Of'n an' of'n in a bad place they would have ropes around the men and pull them out, right up above the danger. But this time the boys knew they'd got to leg it on their own hook; and let me tell you, when you've got five hundred thousand — *feet* that is, board feet — of big pine pitch-poling after you, why you can run all right if there's any run in you. Just heave away your axe and strike a bee-line for the shore, and you won't get there then none too soon for your peace o' mind. Breakin' jams is some uncerting work.

"Well, 't was Rollins's turn to go first, 's I was sayin'. He looked at that key-log and bit his axe in full clip. Did ye ever hear an axe take into wood that's under bustin' strain? Never did? Well, you listen some day, 'f ever you get the chance.

"And Rollins begun his scarf on the under side of the log. That was a right enough thing to do; that was good play; more 'n that, it was fair by Larry. After Rollins got his scarf in all in good shape, Spencer calls him back and sends out Larry.

"Out runs Larry, skippin' and swearin', his kerchief tails flying, and all the boys lookin' on to see him go. A turrible reckless fellow was that Larry. And either he did n't stop to think, or else he did n't care, for the fust thing that he done was to put in his scarf on the *upper* side of that log.

"What 's the trouble with *that?* All the trouble in the *world*, I tell ye, seein' his life might hang on a quarter of a secont! If he 'd 'a' kep' on in Rollins's scarf, that log when it cracked would 'ave

cr-r-r-a-a-*acked*! He'd ha' heard it split-
tin' long enough to ha' got a start before
the jam did. Cuttin' in on the top-side
weakened it too sudden. When the log
broke, it just *bust*.

"Well, then she hauled!

"And by Judas' hemp, an' two select-
men, a yoke of oxen, an' an old snag
throwed in, but p'raps that wa'n't no sight
to see! And to hear, too! Every lad in
sight raised a yell, and those on shore
danced and flung up their hats. And
those on the logs they cut and run like
the *re*cess bell had rung and they did n't
want to be late in. *And* the logs they
started, jumping and squealing and thrashing and grinding, like seventeen sawmills
runnin' full-blast of a Sunday. You never
hearn anything in *your* life like a big jam
of logs let loose. You ain't no idee of the
noise and hubbub one of them will make
when she hauls.

"The men got a pretty good start, but
for all o' that they was tumbled in amongst
the logs and used pretty rough. Two or
three of 'em had to lay down in the cracks

of the laidge and let the logs roll over 'em; but they managed to cling a-holt of the alders, and they all got out 'ceptin' Larry.

"He was quicker'n *three* cats, Larry was, but he wa'n't quite up to the gait them logs set him, just flyin' through the air and up-endin' every which way. And o' course he had the wust chance; that's what he bid for. They tell the story different about Larry. Some says that he made a laidge all right, and a big log squirled and caught him, and they see a red streak just like you'd hit a mosquito there. But what *I* see was that he was on the jam a-runnin', and a big pine lept an' struck him in the back. Head and heels met in the air as it flung him clean. And he fell amongst the logs and they rid over him. But we never see no more of Larry Connors. He said he was goin' to break that jam, if he went to hell for it, and he broke it all right enough."

So that was all there was to it. A brave man — a great dare — a wager won, or lost, as you will — and then all is snuffed out as irrecoverably as the flame of a candle.

They looked for the body far and near, but there was nothing to be found. Babb was the head contractor of the drive that year, and he took charge of the dead man's kit. I have been told that when it was overhauled before being packed to send out to his friends, the men stood round in silence, not so much curious as respectful, wondering how that little bag of worthless duffle turned out on a blanket to be sorted by the head man kneeling beside it could be all that was left of so brave a man as Larry; silent for the most part, or when they did speak, speaking briefly and to the point; for they could not forget that saying of old Jack Mann's, that " Larry was so fond of stealing that when he could n't get anything else he would steal the stocking off from one foot and put it on the other."

" Says one: ' If you find a knife with a boot-leg sheath, it 's mine; Larry borried it mebbe.'

" And another says : ' I 'm short two pair o' socks, blue yarn footed down with gray, lookin' like that pair there.'

"And another and another steps up with his claim.

"So they laid out all the things that was called for. And there was a cardigan marked 'Newell,' and a vest with a handkerchief in it marked 'Myra Spencer,' and other things that did n't seem rightly to belong to his folks. And all the boys looked on it as a judgment on swearing.

"You see there *is* such things as judgments. Never knew a man to say that God Almighty could n't drownd him but he went and got drownded within the hour. There was one up to Telos Cut was rode under by two logs just as soon as he said it. And there was one down to the Gray Rock of Abol, slipped off 'n a perfectly safe place and went downstream like lead, and him a good swimmer. And there was John Goddard's barn that he said he built so firm that the Almighty could n't fetch wind enough to shake it. He 'd had two blow down before that, and he built that one to stand. And then there came a harricane that just sifted that barn into toothpicks, and eight good driving-bo'ts in it, but they never found hide nor hair of 'em. And then there was Larry. Them 's judgments.

" Did n't no one ever find no sign of him? M-m-m-no! That is, *we* did n't. He just went out like the smoke of a dand'li'n blossom; did n't leave no trace. But next spring, when Lewey Ketchum an' Joe Dimon was up on their spring hunt arter bears, down by the Big Eddy,—that's good three mile below the Dry Way; *you* know, you ben there times enough,—in back mebbe a quarter of a mile from the eddy, in open secont growth, I heerd tell that they found a huming skull, and it had the marks of bears' teeth on it.

" They was skinnin' a bear at the time that they 'd just taken out o' their trap, and Joe he sa'ntered off in the woods while Lewey finished off the skin. And bime-by he sung out, ' Lewey — Lewey, there 's the funniest skull here you ever see; awful round it is.'

" ' Lucivee,¹ I guess,' says Lewey, keepin' right on at the skin ; ' they 've got the roundest skull of anything.'

¹ That is, loup-cervier, or Canada lynx, but the hunters pronounce it lucivee or loucerfee.

"' But its front teeth are flat,' sings out Joe.

"' Then it's a *man*,' says Lewey, and he goes and looks.

" And he saw that it had one front tooth gone just like Larry, so they had n't no great of a doubt who it was *to*. They stuck it up in the fork of a tree and spotted a line in to it, so's his friends could find it again if they wanted it, and that's the last that ever I heerd of it."

After this manner the man who broke the jam at the Dry Way came finally, as a bare and eyeless skull, — that blaspheming skull that once had a tongue in it, — to sit like some foul bird in a tree-fork through wintry storms; wherefore the men who had known him felt that even the judgment which had fallen upon him was insufficient, and this strange dismemberment was by the hand of God ordained as a warning against profane swearing. No wonder that they thought his ghost unquiet, and that even on a hot June day it might be out in a red felt hat for a stroll along the Dry Way.

III

HYMNS BEFORE BATTLE

HYMNS BEFORE BATTLE [1]

THE golden noon of a young June day, and fourteen strong men swinging down the carry-path to the "putting-in place;" on each man's shoulder his heavy peavey, clanking its iron jaw as he jolted over rocks and hollows; on each man's feet heavy shoes, studded, heel and sole, with inch-long calks of sharpened steel; on each man's body rags and tatters, worn and weathered from their first monotony of aniline and shoddy into gear indescribably barbarous and fantastic.

[1] This story is reprinted from the *Bangor Daily Commercial*, 1897, at the request of several who have desired its republication among these later stories. Though true in spirit, it does not deal with an actual occurrence at the place named, and therefore is not entitled to admission among these matter-of-fact stories. And yet the owner of another "Nancy," the late Roderick R. Park, when contractor of the Mattawamkeag Drive, used sometimes to call his men off for a dance just like this one, and the good old tune of "Roy's Wife" was known wherever he and his fiddle went.

There was a jam forming below on the Horse Race, — a great upreared mass of logs, like a pile of gigantean jackstraws or the side-swath of a cyclone, where all the wreck is flung, up-ended, interlaced, triply bound and welded, a confusion which seemed inextricable. And volunteers were called to pick the jam.

These were the men, whose armed heels smote fire from the rocks, whose peavies jangled a battle-note, whose short step lengthened to a stride as they saw the river sweeping past and their boats before them, saw the rapids race at the tail of Ambajemackomas and heard on the up-stream draught of air the ominous war of a full flood growling on the Horse Race below, and (either you dread it or it draws you, when you hear the River calling so) came swinging down the carry in haste to meet their foe. It is a pretty sight to see a phalanx of picked watermen rally, as if by bugle call, to face their ancient enemy, the River.

Yet there, in sight of the river, one of them fell out.

"Ho, hi! See here!" he called to those ahead.

The fourteen men with peavies on their shoulders, clustering together, stood stock-still, like old herons round a fishing-pool, their necks craned over, and gazed at something in the damp, black soil.

"Gee whipperty!" said one, "that there's a woman's track!"

Then, as if contradicted, though no one spoke, — "Yes, sir, that is! There's been a woman here."

Women were unknown in that place at that season. Yet there, under the over-arch of an alder, was a slender footprint. They could tell you to-day, those men, though it is twenty years since, just how long and how wide was that woman's track, carelessly imprinted in the mud beside the carry-path.

Very unchivalrous the world counts these woodsmen; — very little the world knows about their ways and romances, for nowhere does romance bear a more fragrant blossom or bloom so long. The sprig of cedar, many years preserved, because with it a woman crowned an act of daring; the wild flower, pressed in the crumpled corner of a greasy pocketbook, because a woman called it beautiful; the chance track in the roadway where a week before an unknown woman stepped, kept from obliteration just because she was a woman, — no line of life that men follow to-day comes so close to the high mark of mediæval chivalry with its superb faith in womankind, regardless of the faults of individual women.

But the life is rough? So surely was chivalry! Rougher than we know for. Its faith saved it; and what grew into mari-olatry in the past is still, in the unromantic present, the better part of many other rough men's religion.

"Yes, sir," said the bearded man; "there was a woman here wunst. Jee-e-e-roozlum, there wuz!"

Confronted by this evidence of a woman's presence, his speech underwent a sudden censorship, and, like rags in a broken window, any inoffensive word was stuffed in to fill the gaps.

" There was; gee-e-e-whittaker, there wuz! It's somethin' to make account of. The wangan chist's this end the carry, and there ain't nothin' can't wait. Hike out old Nancy, and let's break her down."

The speaker was boss of his crew, a man possessed of a little authority over those below him and of more over those above him, who had learned to let him take his own way without meddling; for he was one of those men who, discountenancing the maritime maxim, can break orders and defy owners. It has always been the glory of the West Branch Drive that it had so many such men, every one of whom placed the welfare of those logs above his own life, could have handled the whole drive if there were need, and whose insubordination would never have gone so far as to endanger the least part of their trust. No matter how mutinously they spoke, they never failed to be where they were needed, and that was all P. L. D. asked of them.

There is neither time nor room for fiddles on the drive, but this man had wanted Nancy, and he carried Nancy. If he had wanted the moon, he would have put it in the wangan chest·just as boldly. And now, when called to pick off a jam, he coolly halts his men in the face of danger and death — because the occasion is notable — to have a scrape at the old fiddle.

In the faces of some there is questioning what John Ross will say. Whom he rebukes.

"What 'll John Ross say? Don't *care* what John Ross 'll say! Ain't this a free country? What did old Jack Mann say to *his* boss when he knocked off at noon with all his crew because it looked like sprinklin'? — that he 'd 'a sight ruther have the good-will of a whole crew than of one man, any day.' 'N' so 'd I! John Ross ain't a-runnin' this crew now; *I* be! There ain't nothin' in partic'lar 'bout a little side jam that can't wait. Stick up your darts, boys; rowse a boat out, an' all hands bow to pardners."

In a trice they were ready. The peavies plunged their iron beaks into the earth, the driving-boat turned bottom up in a twinkling, and while the boss was still groping in the wangan chest for his fiddle-case, the two supplest men had unbuckled and cast aside their spiked driving-shoes. It was a dance on the drive — a dance by proxy ; for the pitchy, flat bottom of a driving-boat is an area too limited for a general engagement. So while the fiddler sawed and tightened his strings, and the bare-footed dancers sprung their knees to get them in condition, the audience disposed itself to watch.

The fiddle tuned, the fiddler seated, he touches the horse-hair to his cheek, then holds the bow upright and Nancy tucked beneath his chin, waiting for them to call the tune.

"' Money Musk ' ! "

"' Fisher's Hornpipe '! "

"' Irish Washerwoman ' ! "

" Somethin' 't we sing out in the States," cries a dissenting basso; "give us a real Christian tune ! "

There is rough water below them and a jam to pick; and — are they moved to sing hymns of prayer and praise ?

O innocent, the fiddler knows them

better. He bends his head a moment to catch the humor of his audience moved to retrospection by the sight of a woman's footprint, and away whisk jigs and "pennyroyals" while the expectant dancers stand agape.

Up and down plays his wrist, in and out works his elbow, forward and back sways his body ; he treads his foot; a musical ecstasy carries him beyond the bounds of his own mean accomplishments, and he plays with fervor what his men have called for — a most Christian song. It begins, —

> "I 'm lonesome since I crossed the hill,
> And o'er the moor and valley."

And they sang. Of course they sang, — bass and tenor, how they sang, for they all knew that, — sang till the clearer voices floated high above the slender birch-tops and the bass swam midway in the clear June sunshine, and beneath, mingling with the roll of the rapids, rumbled the undertone of those who could not sing, yet would not refuse to try. It came like rain in drought, freshening dusty foliage and

slaking the thirst of parching hillsides —
this most Christian song of women remembered in the face of danger.

> "The bee shall honey taste no more,
>   The dove become a ranger,
>   The falling waves shall cease to roar,
>   Ere I shall seek to change her.
>   The vows we register'd above
>   Shall ever cheer and bind me,
>   In constancy to her I love,
>   The girl I 've left behind me."

The logs slipped past by twos and threes
and half-dozens, going to throw themselves
upon the abattis of the ever-increasing jam
below. And still the fiddler bent above
his fiddle. Young men have sweethearts,
older men have wives, and once more the
bow is laid to the catgut, to draw from it
a tribute to the wives at home.

"Roy's Wife of Valdevally" nods the
bow-paddle to the stroke-oar. They did
not know the words, nor that it had words,
nor that they were not altogether a compliment, — that lay all in the title, — but
the fine old tune of "Roy's Wife of Aldi-
valloch" was known wherever Nancy felt

the bow. It had been played many times before on that river, though never when John Ross was waiting for a crew.

That ended, once more the bow hugged the fiddle. To young men, sweethearts; to their seniors, wives; but men old enough to handle the bow of a driving-boat have children and homes as well, and the fiddler played once more while John Ross waited.

Up through the tangle of undergrowth by the river's edge, hastening from the jam below, jingling his dippers as he ran, puffed and sweated the luncheon-boy, with orders to "swear them into a two-forty; for it had caught on at the middle and formed clear across the river, was rolling up all the time, and would hold till everything underground froze stiff" (so the message ran), "if they did n't shove a crew down double · quick and break the jam; and why in — in all hemlock, had n't they been there long before?"

An order enjoining unlimited, idiomatic, artistic swearing is a commission of honor to any luncheon-boy, and this one, as he posted up the drivers' path by the river-

bank, was marshaling his vocabulary so as
to do him credit, when, though full of his
errand, he heard the fiddle, soft and sweet,
— for the bow itself crooned the words to
silent listeners, —

"In mansions or palaces, where'er I roam,
  Be it never so humble, there's no place like home."

The luncheon-boy loitered along at a
walk, then sauntered, and finally, in spite
of his hot haste, waited till the last slow
stave had sung itself away to an echo.

" Middle jam," said he, shamefully neg-
lecting the opportunity for elegant profanity ; " everything piling up chock-full.
Run down lively ; them 's John Ross's
orders."

Fourteen men sprang to their feet and
ran out the batteaus ; the fiddle shut itself up in the case ; the peavies leaped into
the boats ; oars, axes, paddles, and all flew
into position, and the two driving-boats,
fully manned, with bowmen and steersmen
standing in their places, darted out into
the swirling current that tails down from
Ambajemackomas. Behind them were

songs of sweetheart, wife, and home ; and ahead, around the bend whence the up-stream draught of air brought the growl of the rapids, Death and Danger sat waiting for them on the middle jam. Were their chances for life and victory less for that quarter hour's devotion at the one shrine all woodsmen worshipfully recognize, — the memory of home and woman?

IV

THE DEATH OF THOREAU'S GUIDE

THE DEATH OF THOREAU'S GUIDE

THE strangest monument a man ever had
in sacred memory, — a pair of old boots.
For a token of respect and admiration, love
and lasting grief, — just a pair of old river-
driver's boots hung on the pin-knot of a
pine. Big and buckled; bristling all over
the sole with wrought steel calks; gashed
at the toes to let the water out; slashed
about the tops into fringes with the tally
of his season's work, less only the day
which saw him die; reddened by water;
cracked by the sun, — worn-out, weather-
rotting old boots, hanging for years on the
pine-tree, disturbed by no one. The river-
drivers tramped back and forth beneath
them, a red-shirted multitude; they boated
along the pond in front and drove their
logs past, year after year; they looked at
the tree with the big cross cut deep in its

scaly bark, and always left the boots hanging on the limb. They were the Governor's boots, Joe Attien's boots, they belonged to Thoreau's guide.[1]

The pine-tree had seen the whole. It was old and it was tall. Its head stretched up so high that it could look over the crest of Grand Pitch, tremendous fall though it is, right up where Grand Falls come churning down to their final leap into Shad Pond. It had been looking up the river in the sunshine of that summer morning and had seen the whole, — the overloaded boat that set out to run the falls, the wreck in the rapids, the panic of the crew, the men struggling among logs and rocks, the brave attempt at rescue, and the dead, drowned bulk, which had once been the Governor, as it was tumbled down over the Grand Pitch into the pond below. The pine-tree had stood guard over it for days, and when, from its four days

[1] Thoreau spells the name "Aitteon;" I have preferred the form found on his tombstone, "Attien," because it indicates both the pronunciation and the derivation. For it is not Indian, but the French Étienne, or Stephen.

in the grave of the waters, it rose again,
the pine-tree still kept watch over it, until,
on the sixth morning, the searchers found
it there. "And when they found his body
they cut a cross into a tree by the side
of the pond, and they hung up his boots
in the tree and they stayed there always,
because everybody knew that they was the
Governor's boots."

If ever Henry David Thoreau showed
himself lacking in penetration, it was when
he failed to get the measure of Joseph
Attien. True, Joe was young then — he
never lived to be old; yet a man who, dying at forty-one, is so long remembered,
must have shown some signs of promise
at twenty-four.[1] But Thoreau hired an
Indian to be aboriginal. One who said
"By George!" and made remarks with a
Yankee flavor was contrary to his hypo-
thesis of what a barbarian ought to be. It

[1] The newspapers said he was thirty-five when he died,
but his gravestone says plainly, "forty years and seven
months." It is interesting to learn that one who lived
so well and died so generously was born on Christmas
Day.

did not matter that this was the sort of man who gave up his inside seat and rode sixty miles on the top of the stage in the rain that a woman might be sheltered ; — all the cardinal virtues without aboriginality would not have sufficed Mr. Thoreau for a text. He missed his opportunity to tell us what manner of man this was, and so Joe Attien's best chance of being remembered lies, not in having been Henry Thoreau's guide on a brief excursion, but in being just brave, honest, upright Joseph Attien, a man who was loved and lamented because he had the quality of goodness. " His death just used the men all up," said a white riverman years afterward ; " after that some of the best men wa'n't good for anything all the rest of the drive."

I could give, as I have gleaned it here and there, the testimony to his worth, the statements of one and another that he was not only brave but good, an open-hearted, patient, forbearing sort of a man, renowned for his courage and skill in handling a boat, but loved for his mild justness. " He was just like a father to us," said a white man who had been in his boat. Thirty-three years after his death I heard a head lumberman, who also had served two years in his boat, a very silent man, break out into voluble reminiscence at merely seeing Joe Attien's picture. But there is a story, indisputably authentic, which shows better than anything else the largeness of the man.

He had been slandered by a white man whom he had thought his friend, in a way which not only caused him distress of mind, but was calculated to interfere materially with his election to the office of tribal governor, the most coveted honor within an Indian's grasp, and that year elective for the first time.[1] The incident occurred just

[1] His epitaph is wrong in asserting that he inherited the title of governor. The office had been a life-office, hereditary in the Attien family, who were chiefs ; but at Joseph's father's death it was made annual and elective. Joseph Attien won his elections by popular vote against great opposition, and he carried seven out of the eight elections held up to the time of his death. The eighth — by the intervention of the so-called " Special Law," passed by the state to reduce the friction between the parties — was the New Party's first election, none of Joseph Attien's party, the Old Party, or Conservatives, voting that year.

before his first election in 1862, — for he was governor seven times. Hurt to the quick, he avoided his former friend, yet said nothing. When he discovered that the false accusation had arisen from a wholly innocent and most natural mistake, without a word in his own justification, leaving the charge to stand undenied, he renewed the old friendship, and his friend never knew what just cause he had given for resentment till, years after Joe's death, it was accidentally revealed by one who had heard the misunderstanding explained. Such was the man.

If you ask the men who were there at the time how Joseph Attien died, they will never suggest that it was accident or the hand of God. More or less emphatically, according to their natures and the vividness of their recollection, they will say right out, " Dingbat Prouty did it ; it was Dingbat Prouty drownded Joe Attien." They will cheerfully admit that this is not a man to be spoken of slightingly, because he is a great waterman ; but upon this point

there is only one opinion,—that he forced
Joe Attien to run a bad place against his
better judgment, for the mere sake of
showing off. " He pushed himself in."
—" He had n't no business in that boat
at all." —" Prouty drownded Joe Attien,
everybody who was there says so." —
" He had n't no business in that boat and
did n't belong there anyway, but he said he
was going to run them falls, and he did
run 'em."

It is very hard to tell a true story, and
the more one knows about the facts, the
harder it is to make a story of them. Here
was a simple tale of how the inordinate am-
bition of one man to win a name for himself brought grief upon the whole drive.
The next turn of the kaleidoscope gave a
wholly different combination. For I took
what I had gathered to John Ross himself.
" Is this straight?" And he said: " No;
you are all wrong there. Prouty belonged
in that boat; he had been bowman of it
about two days. It was my orders for them
to go down and pick a jam on the Heater,
and they were going. I was right there and

saw the whole of it, and I never blamed Prouty."

But why, then, should the men have blamed him ? No exculpation could be more complete than this. There is no appeal from what John Ross says he ordered and saw executed. Why do not the men know this ? Instead of telling a simple tale, are we undertaking to square the mental circle ? For, with nearly two hundred men close at hand, it seems preposterous that the facts should not have become generally known ; it is still more incredible to suppose that, thinking independently, they could all have reached the same false conclusion; but that, having been cross-examined in all sorts of ways for four and thirty years, they should never have varied from their first error is inconceivable. Why do the men still hold Charles Prouty responsible, if he was not to blame ?

From being a study of facts, the story turns into a question of psychology. Why is it that when one has been looking at red too long he sees green and keeps on seeing green, even when there is no green there?

That is the clue. A man does not get a
name like "Dingbat" and keep it all his
life for nothing. Therefore, after the men
had gazed fixedly upon the commanding
excellence of Joseph Attien; after they had
seen him pass beyond their ken, " all the
trumpets," as it were, " sounding for him
on the other side;" when they turned away
and looked at the man whom fate had
elected to stand beside him that day, what
would one expect them to see by contrast?
Green! very green! And to keep right
on seeing — *green!*

Having affirmed the worth of Joseph
Attien and the warm esteem in which all
held him, it remains to show how, because
he was placed in too sharp a contrast with
such a man, Charles Prouty incurred a blame
which his chief says was none of his.

We come now to the story. Chance
gave to it a fitting frame — grand scenery,
bright sunshine, a date of distinction, the
eye of the master. You are never to forget that up on a log-jam, just below where
this happened, stood himself — John Ross.

He ordered the boat down; he saw it go; he sent another to the rescue; he reported this to me; it stands authenticated. But what the men saw and felt, that which is unofficial, that which represents the current of the story and carries us on to the end, I gathered for myself among them.

On the drive there is no distinction of days. Holidays or Sundays, the drivers know no difference; one week's end and the next one's beginning are all the same to them. The Fourth of July now is marked for them by no other suitable recognition than extremely early rising.

But it used not so to be. In the old days, when it was a point of pride to have the logs in boom by the last of June, the men were free to celebrate on the Fourth. To them the Fourth of July was the greatest day of all the year. Like boys just out of school, they were free from work, free from restraint, free to make just as much noise as they pleased, and, having plenty of money in their pockets wherewith to purchase all sorts of a good time, they

enjoyed a glorious liberty. The Fourth
was never a quiet day in Bangor, if the
drives were in the boom.

However, the year of our Lord 1870 is
distinctly chronicled as one of the most un-
eventful ever known; nothing at all going
on but a church levee across the river in
Brewer, so that the police loafed out the
Fourth in weary and unwonted idleness.
The drives were late that year, so very late
that, though the head of the West Branch
Drive was some miles downstream, the
rear of it rested on the Grand Falls of the
Indian Purchase. The hands had been
leaving the day before, so as to get home
for the Fourth; the water was falling; the
whole drive was belated and short-handed;
the head men were worrying; no one had
any time to remember that it was a legal
holiday.

That is, no one remembered it except
the Chronic Shirk. His rights had been
assailed, and, having found a Temporary
Cripple, who could not escape by flight
from his unwelcome company, he insisted
on arguing the case, and volleyed back his

opinions of working on a legal holiday with an explosiveness which reminded one of the reports of a bunch of fire-crackers.

It was " Rip — rip — rip — *bang!* But he did n't *like* this workin' on a Fourth er Ju*ly!* The Declaration of Independuns had said — that it was a man's right — on the Fourth er July — to git as tight as Lewey's cow ; and he did rip — rip — rip — *object* — to bein' defrauded out of his constitoot'nal rights ! "

He was a sun-baked, stubble-faced fellow; less troubled with clothes than with the want of patches, but with shirt and skin about one color where the sun had toned them to each other around the more ancient rents ; and he sat in a niche in the log-jam, expectorating tobacco forcibly and to great distances, and swore voluminously about his ill-luck in not being somewhere else. Just then he had nothing to do. He was an expert at picking out jobs where there was nothing to do. This time he was waiting for his mate, who had gone for an axe, and not a stroke of work had he done since his mate left him. There it was, a bright sunny morning about seven o'clock, a good time to work, and the logs ricked up like jackstraws on both sides of the falls; the whole river in that confusion which the rear has to clean up and leave tidy; plenty of work for this fellow to do with his peavey in picking off singles and rolling in little handfuls caught along the edges, and helping to do his share of the setting to rights; but instead, he sat on a log-jam in the sun, and spat more vigorously and swore more violently as it grew upon him how ill the world was using him in making him work on the Fourth of July.

The Cripple, unable to escape, tried to divert him from his melancholy. "Well, Tobias Johnson's bo't got down all right," he remarked.

Tobias Johnson and his crew had but just run the Blue Rock Pitch. It was to see the boats go down that the Cripple had crawled out upon the logs. The water being very bad that morning, what Tobias Johnson had done was bound to be a topic of conversation all that hot day among little

groups of men working on the logs. Even
the Shirk ought to have whirled at such a
glittering conversational lure. Instead he
sulked.

"I'd be rip — rip — ripped, if I was
seen runnin' these here falls to-day. It's
a damned shame to have to work on the
Fourth er July anyway. Head men that
knowed beans from bedbugs would ha'
had the whole jim-bang drive in long
ago," and he exploded a whole bunch of
crackers on the heads of the offending
contractors of the drive. "Here we be
a-swillin' sow-belly an' Y. E. B.'s,[1] an'
down to Bangor, don't I know jes' 's well
as can be, Deacon Spooner has brought
up a thousand pounds o' salmon to Low's
Market, an' is reportin' all about the sun-
stroke to the schoolhouse, an' the camp-
meetin' they are gettin' up down to Whisgig
on Shoo-Fly, an' salmon enough for all
hands an' the cook."

[1] That is, yellow-eyed beans. Pork and beans are the
river-driver's staple of diet, as well as the lumberman's,
and not as much relished in midsummer as in the colder
season.

(Deacon Spooner was a sort of summer Santa Claus, who purveyed imaginary information and real Penobscot River salmon. He was held in high local esteem, but he went out of print about this time, and the great volley of oaths which the Shirk shot off at the merry and inoffensive deacon, though they may not account for his disappearance, would provide good reason for looking for him among the damned.)

The Cripple tried to get away, but he was too closely followed. Then, deciding that talking was better than listening, he took the reins of conversation. " Bi must have found it awful rough water," said he. " Don't believe there 'll be not another bo't attempt it to-day, with the water slacking so. Say, did you hear that yisterday Joe Attien tried to git Con Murphy to leave Tobias's crew an' come into his bo't? An' Con said he liked his own crew, an' did n't want to change, not even to be in Joe's bo't. I heerd that he got Ed Conley out of Lewey Ketchum's bo't, now Lewey 's left the drive. Speaks pretty well for Tobias, though, don't it ?"

The discontented one turned impartially from Deacon Spooner and damned Tobias.

"Jim Hill!" said the other, "how them logs has took to runnin'! They're goin' it high, wide, an' lively. That stops all bo't capers for one while. Any bo't that had it in mind to rival Bi Johnson had better think twice about it before they get out into this mix-up on slack water. Guess our fun's up an' I mought's well be crawlin' back to camp."

"Guess I mought's well stay right here where I be," said the Shirk; "John Ross is up there on that dry jam east side, an' I'd jes''s soon be where I can keep an eye on him."

The Cripple made a few painful, hobbling steps over the logs and had reached the crest of the jam, when he turned with his hand shading his eyes and looked down toward the Blue Rock Pitch, where a boat was drawn up on the shore and the crew stood waiting.

"Say, though," he shouted to the Shirk, trying to make himself heard above the water, " looks like they was talkin' about runnin' after all! Who is it? make 'em out?"

The grumbler put up his head cautiously to make sure that John Ross was attending to his own business, before he ran briskly to the peak of the jam, and announced that it was that ding-ding-danged Injun, Joe Attien; could tell him by his bigness.

" Hain't he the perfect figure of a man, though!" broke in the other in admiration; "pity his heft keeps him from his rightful place in the bow."

Joe Attien weighed two hundred and twenty-five and, because of his great weight and strength, always captained his boat from the stern, although in running down quick water the bow is the place of honor.

The leisurely one, having made sure that he was getting the right man, proceeded to curse Joe Attien and all his forbears. Then he sat down upon the logs and resumed his original lamentation. " Now down Bangor way to-day they'd be doin' somp'n wuth lookin' at—hoss races an' bo't races an'"—

" Joe 'd be in the canoe race sure," interrupted the other.

"Not by a long chalk!" said the grumbler; "don't you see he 's governor agin? Don't you rec'lect that last time, when they made him a ding-danged, no-good judge, an' him one of the best paddles in the tribe, a rip — rip — rip — splitting good man on a paddle, all because he was a ding-dang-donged governor?"

The other man admitted the cogency of the argument. "But say," said he, "that 's the real thing there. Ain't that Dingbat talkin' up to Joe?"

They watched the rapid, incisive movements of a slender, agile young fellow, outlined against Joe's bulk. "Dinged little weasel," muttered the grumbler, identifying him; "so durn spry 't he don't cast no shadder!"

Then he relapsed once more into his reflective mood. "Now down Bangor way now, you bet, — oh, hoss races an' bo't races an' canoe races, an' 'Torrent' and 'Delooge' a-squirtin' out in the Square, an' cirkiss an' greased pig, an' tub races an' velocerpede races, — there 'll be somp'n down there to-day wuth lookin' at, an' up here nothin' but this dod-blasted ol' river an' a ding-dang passel o' logs !' "

" Say," said the other, " I can't quite make that out yet. I ain't a-catchin' on to that performance. There 's McCausland an' Tomer an' Joe Solomon an' Curran an' Conley, they all belong — but where 's Steve Stanislaus ? An' that little Dingbat — what 's he doin' with a paddle there ? "

" Wants Joe to run the falls."

" Well, but he ain't in Joe's bo't ! "

" Course not, little rumscullion ! That 's it ! He 's failed to get his own crew in, most like, an' now he 's stumpin' Joe to take him along o' his crew. You watch an' see him do it. He ain't a-goin' to let Bi Johnson have the name of bein' the only man that dares to run these falls to-day, not if he can help it. He 'll shake the rafters o' heaven but he 'll show us that he 's every bit as good a waterman as Tobias Johnson."

" What makes him light on Joe ? and where 's Steve ? "

The men did not know as yet that the day before, when the crews reorganized at the Lower Lakes, Steve· Stanislaus, who was Joe Attien's friend and cousin and physical counterpart, had left Joe's boat. But all sorts of low cunning being readable to the Shirk, he was not at loss for an explanation.

"Well, don't you see, he's cut Steve out some ways. Joe handlin' stern, that gives him a chance to go in the bow, and that's right on the way to a bo't of his own, and what he could n't get with no other man. He don't ship to be no midshipman in the maulin' they are goin' to git. He's figgerin' how to put hisself at a premum as a crack man."

"Reel Dingbat trick," muttered the other. "Joe knows that this ain't no runnin' water to-day ; just wicked to try to run here, the way things is now."

"Don't want to, don't have to," retorted the swearer, for once omitting the garnish of his speech. And it was more true than most epigrams. Joe's orders to go down with a boat did not imply that he was to

run the Blue Rock Pitch against his judgment. A waterman of his reputation could
dare to be prudent. All the spectators
thought that he intended to take out above
the pitch and carry by. Then they saw
him pick up his long paddle.

The Shirk pricked up his ears and
began to be more cheerful. " Looks like
somp'n was goin' to happen now!" he
chippered. " There they are a-gettin' of
her ready. Now they 're runnin' her out.
There 's Dingbat takin' bow. Wonder
what they are goin' to do with that spare
man? Which one of them rip — rip —
rippin' galoots do you s'pose Joe 'll be
leavin' behind?"

That seventh man in the boat was what
the men never understood ; it gave the
color to the accusation that Prouty pushed
himself in. Seven men is a boat's crew
when working on logs, but in running
dangerous places they carry but six or even
four men. It would seem as if, planning
not to run, Joe had his log-working crew,
and then, changing his mind suddenly,
forgot to leave behind the extra man.

"Gosh! how rough the water is!" said the Cripple; "all choked up with jams both sides, and the logs running to beat hell. They don't stand one chance not in — My soul! — but he's puttin' that spare man in on the lazy seat! Well, what you must do you will do." It was the inbred fatalism of his class, which makes them stoical.

Simultaneously the grumbler fired off a volley of curses which made the air smoke. "Rip — rip — rip — bang! — bang!! If that Go-donged Injun ain't a-shippin' a Maddywamkeag crew!" (In the cant of the river a "Mattawamkeag crew" means all the men a boat will hold.)

The Shirk was fully alive now. He jumped up and took his peavey from the log side of him. "Guess I'll be moseyin' right along down now," he chirped. Then he set out running over the logs at a lively pace, trailing his peavey behind him. He anticipated seeing something fully equal to greased pig and velocipede races.

There was not much to see that time. The catastrophe came at once, before they

were fairly started. The water was very
rough that morning—on a falling driving-
pitch it is always roughest. There was that
crowning current heaped up in the middle
that would push a boat up on the shore;
there were the log-jams making the channels narrow and crooked; there were the
loose logs running free that would elbow
and ram a boat and crowd her off when
she tried to avoid them; there were the
doubtful, treacherous channels, creatures
of the log-jams along the banks and of the
fickle current, new with every differing
condition, never to be fully memorized;
there were the rocks, not less cruel because cushioned with great boils of water;
and there were the boat's own weight and
tremendous momentum. No thorough-
bred waterman will ever undertake to say
how fast a boat can run in a rapid; for he
does not know himself. He says, "Very
fast," and turns the topic to all-day records.

Still the great sharp-nosed boat had as
little cause to apprehend disaster as any
boat could have had. She bore a picked
crew; she obeyed Joe Attien; and she was

a staunch and trusty boat, very wise about all the ways of water. She knew all kinds and how to take them. There were the huge boils, those frightful, brandy-colored boils, streaked full of yellow foam-threads spinning from a hissing centre; and there were the slicks, where a great rock betrayed his lurking-place only by the tail of glassy current below, — safe are such places, for the rock lies above them; and there were the ridgy manes of white water-curls, where the slopes of two great rocks met and rolled the water backward; — but she knew how to take them all; she was prepared for perils on all sides, danger unintermittent, whether she took it slick, or bit into the foam with her long beak, or caught it raw and crosswise beneath her flaring gunwales. What she did not expect was that her peril would come before she had caught the set of the current at all; no one looked for that, not even the Shirk, who was running fast so as to be right on hand when she swamped, and was addressing to them various select remarks not intended to be heard above the roar of the

water, such as, " Guess you got your belly
full this time, old fellow ; " and, " Go it,
boys, you 'll get plumb to hell this trip."
It was nothing to one of his kind that
seven men stood in deadly peril, and the
show of the moment he was craftily neg-
lecting that he might the better witness the
closing spectacle ; but he never dreamed
that it would come as it did.

It was a very simple accident ; the
dragon-fly, with bulging eyes, rustling in
zigzag flight along the river's brink, might
have reported what he saw as well as could
a man. There was the long, lean boat, blue
without and painted white within, lying with
pointed stern and longer, tapering snout,
steeving sharply, like a huge fish half out
of water ; within her the line of red-shirted
men, their finny oars fringing her battered
sides, the stripling Prouty high up in the
bow, too eager to snatch the honors of which
he has won so many fairly since ; then the
row of seated men — ragged red shirts,
sorely weathered ; hard red knuckles, tense
on the oar-butts ; sun-burned faces under
torn brims, or hatless ; sun-scorched eyes,

winking through sun-bleached lashes; all, Yankee and Irishman and Province-man, black-eyed Indian and blue-eyed Indian, waiting on big Joe Attien towering in the stern, confident that what he did would be done right. Seven men, and four were looking backward to the shore and three were facing forward toward the water, four one way and three the other, as if emblematic of the coming moment when they should be divided by three and by four, for life, for death. What they thought and how they felt, who could tell now? but out of all those there, the man's heart which would have been best worth reading was that spare man's on the lazy seat, who knew rough water, and could see ahead, and who had nothing at all to do. If he unbuckled his stout, calked brogans, and slipped them off his feet, who could say whether it was done from fear or from foresight?

Then the poles dip, the long spruce iron-shod poles at bow and stern, the oars sweep shallow water, and, splashing and gritting gravel as they push off, the poles

dipping one side and the other, abreast
and backward, like the long legs of an un-
certain-minded crane-fly, they shove her
out.

And then was their black fate close upon
them : she did not swing to the current ;
she was too heavy ; the crew were raw to
one another and to the boat; bow and stern
did not respond as they always had done
when Steve Stanislaus and Joe handled
boat, as their old crews still say, "just
like one man." Logy and bewildered,
instead of turning promptly to the current,
the old boat let the water catch her under-
neath her side. It shot her straight across
the channel, right among the ugly rocks
on the other shore, close above the Blue
Rock Pitch. Before she could be straightened, the River took her in his giant
hands and smashed her side against a
rock, smote her down with such a crash
that the men along the banks who saw
and heard it cannot be convinced that she
was not wrecked ; and some who saw her
fill so suddenly still declare that her whole
bottom was torn off as you rip the peel

from a mandarin orange. That is not true ; she was not much hurt. But eighteen hundred pounds of boat and men were hurled upon that sunken rock with the full force of the River. The port side buckled fearfully ; the ribs groaned and gave ; the nails screamed as the sharp rock sheared off their heads, and a long yellow shaving, ploughed out of her side, went writhing down the foaming current. Down to the water's edge dipped the upstream gunwale ; in poured the water in a flood, and before she settled squarely, the lifted port side showed that long and ugly scar. What of the shock that sent the man upon the lazy seat reeling backward, that tumbled the men at the oars forward upon their faces, that wrenched their oars from their hands and threw the batteau seats from the cleats and sent the spare man's driving-shoes adrift among the litter of unshipped seats and useless men ? Unmanned, unmanageable, full to the lips of water, and just on the brink of the Blue Rock Pitch, what could the old boat do? Joe dropped his useless pole and took his paddle, but she could not answer to it, and bow-heavy with the weight of water running forward as she felt the incline of the fall, her stern reeling high in air, her crew, disarmed and helpless, crowding on the bowman, she wallowed down that wicked water among rocks and logs.

So much is fairly certain, but beyond this no one seems quite sure ; for I can find no one who saw it. Tobias Johnson's crew could not, not having eyes in the backs of their heads, for they had sprung at once to the rescue in their own boat. The Shirk, who would have been glad to see, was out of the running. In his haste to be on hand, he had tripped himself on his peavey and had been plunged headforemost into a hole in the jam, where, kicking and clawing, he went off like Mother Hoyt's powder-horn. (Cursing his own awkwardness ? No, not a bit ! Damning the men who were struggling in the water, because they had tripped him up and hadn't given him a fair chance to see them die !) Nor did John Ross on his log-jam see it, though he was so near.

" I was on a dry jam right there, but I had kept Levi Hathorn's boat with me in case any one should tumble in or anything should happen, and I sent it down to them — and I don't know any more. I saw that they were going to have a hard time, and — and I turned and looked the other way." (Ladies and gentlemen, — tender-hearted ladies, high-minded gentlemen, — pause and consider whether, standing there, yours would have been the transcendent grace that " turned and looked the other way ! ")

One thing everybody knows, — there were men in that boat who could not swim ; there are such in every boat. The others leaped and swam ; these clung to the boat. And Joe Attien stayed with them, — not clinging as they did, buried in water; not crouching and abject, waiting for the death that faced him, — not a coward now, never, but paddle in hand, because the water ran too deep for pole-hold, standing astride his sunken boat, a big, calked foot upon either gunwale, working to the last ounce that was in him to drive the sunken wreck

and the men clinging to it into some eddy
or cleft of the log-jams before they were
carried down over the Heater and that
thundering fall of the Grand Pitch. It is
the last one sees of Joe Attien, no one has
reported anything after that; one remembers him always as standing high in the
stern of his boat, dying with and for his men.

The Humane Society gives no medals
for rescues made along the river; our men
have nothing to show for anything they
have done; but when all the pæans of
brave deeds are chanted, let some one remember to sing the praises of Tobias Johnson's crew. We do not speak of them —
this is not their day. Enough that when
they saw Joe Attien's boat swamp, they all
leaped into their places and swept out to
the rescue. Man after man they pulled in,
heedless of their own safety. The last one
they caught when they were just on the
verge of the Heater, and then somehow,
overloaded as they were, on the brink of
sure death, they swung in and crept back
to the landing-place.

Ashore they looked over the saved and called the names of the dead. They had three, McCausland and Joe Solomon and Curran. Joe Attien was gone, and Stephen Tomer, an Indian lad, and Edward Conley of Woodstock, and Dingbat Prouty. They still hoped for these, — hope dies hard, and they knew how difficult it is to drown a man who resolutely prefers to try his chances of being hanged. So they and all who had flocked in to them at the flying rumor of disaster took up pick-poles, pickaroons, peavies, whatever might be used to save a living man or to recover the body of a drowned one, and set off down the drivers' path which skirts the falls.

There was little hope of finding Joe. When they saw him go, they all understood that, dead or alive, they would find him with his men. But Dingbat had been seen swimming strongly. If the logs had not crushed him nor the rocks broken him, he might yet be picked up in some inshore cove, where the eddy played, clinging to the alders, too fordone to pull himself out, but still alive.

They searched well, and they searched some time before they found him, — for I had it from one who was there,— and when they did discover him, it was the rescuers who were scant of breath.

"Ga-w-d! but don't he seem to be takin' it easy!" said one.

For a man who had just been through what he had been through, he certainly was taking it very easy. He was sitting on a log out in an eddy, a great hulling-machine log, peeled by the rocks in rapids, with tatters of bark hanging to its scarred sides, bitten to the quick by the ledges, broomed at the ends by being tumbled over falls. There in the eddy it was drifting, because it was too big to be dislodged until some driver prodded it out and over the Grand Pitch. Unable to escape, it went sailing round and round, sometimes butting other logs and ramming the weaker ones out into the rapids, sometimes nosing up against the line of the current, and always drawing back again into its quiet haven, swimming slowly, but swinging often, ever a little beyond the line of the bushes, ever a little inside the line of the current. The falls-spume gathered in clots against the side farthest from the eddy's vortex, and the torrent, as it rushed past, threw up wavelets that lapped its flanks. There in the warm morning sunshine, wet as a drowned rat, his hair plastered over his sharp-cut face, and the wrinkles round his nose showing clearer than common, sat the missing bowman, dripping from every edge and elbow, but stolidly sucking his pipe.

"Well, I call that *nerve!*" remarked one of the rescuers, viewing him from behind a screen of bushes. He appreciated the self-command it took for a man considerably more than half drowned and entirely soaked to get out his old pipe, dig her clean, and clamp her under his spiked shoe to dry while he peeled his wet tobacco down to the solid heart of it, got out his matches from his little water-tight vial, and filled and lit her up. They admired his young bravado and waited a moment watching him, as, theatrically unconscious of their presence, which he well enough observed, he drew at his pipe and swung with the eddy, his shadow now falling to the front, now to the rear.

"Ain't he a James Dickey-bird!" said another beneath his breath.

Then Dingbat overdid the matter.

"Where's that damned Injun?" he demanded, suddenly acknowledging their presence.

The ichor of swift resentment coursed through their veins; already it was settled in their minds who was responsible for this disaster. Here he was, safe enough, having saved himself; Joe Attien was dead trying to save his crew. As the lightning-flash sometimes photographs indelibly the objects nearest where it strikes, so on the minds of these men that unfeeling question branded forevermore the pictures that stood for those two lives, — Dingbat floating at his ease in the eddy, having looked out for himself, Joe Attien drowned and battered and lost among logs and ledges, willing to lose himself if he might save his crew. They have never forgotten, never will forget that difference. To this day, when you ask one of them who was there at the time how Joe Attien died, this contrast leaps before him, and he says that Dingbat Prouty did it.

The rapids give place to river meadows, the meadows grow into salt shore-marshes, the marshes lose themselves at the verge of ocean, and a mist creeps up out of the sea. Time levels and softens all, and draws a veil of haze across to hide what is unpleasantly harsh. So be it! Let all that is unworthy, low, or mean be blotted out, provided that the lights we steer by, the beacons across the wide waste waters, be not dimmed;—leave us, O Time, the memory of men like this!

I was a tiny child when Joe Attien died. He had been a familiar friend, and often, no doubt, he fondled me as he did his own babies. But I do not remember him. Instead I recall—not clearly, though I somehow know that it was they—the delegation of Indians who came down to ask my father where they should go to look for his body. They were tall, and I looked through their legs as between tree-trunks, and the shadow of grief on their dark faces made them like the heavy tops of the pine-trees, trees of mournfulness and sighing.

"Spos'n' gov'nor could got pole-holt, she could saved 'em."

And, "She could saved it herself gov'nor, 'cause she strong man and could swim, but she want to preservation crew."

So my father pondered the problem, and told them where to look for the body. "A brick would swim in that water, it is so strong," said he. "The governor was a heavy man, but unless he is jammed under logs or wedged between rocks, he will be carried right down over Grand Pitch. As soon as the current slackens, it will drop him and he will sink in shallow water at the inlet to the pond. It is hot weather now, and the water being shoal there, by the time you can get up river the body will have risen; you will find it in the upper end of Shad Pond."

It all came out as he had predicted. The body of Edward Conley had been

picked up above the falls several days before, but the two Indians they found together in Shad Pond on Sunday, the sixth
day. They took both the bodies ashore,
and where they landed they cut a deep
cross into a tree; and because they could
not treat lightly anything which had belonged to so brave a man, Joe Attien's
boots they hung upon a limb of the tree.
There the river-drivers left them till they
wasted away, a strange but sincere memorial of a good man.

V

THE GRAY ROCK OF ABOL

THE GRAY ROCK OF ABOL

"The region of which I speak is a dreary region . . . by the borders
of the river . . . and there is no quiet there, nor silence. . . .
The waters of the river . . . palpitate forever and forever beneath
the red eye of the sun. . . . But there is a boundary to their
realm — the boundary of the dark, horrible, lofty forest. . . .

"And mine eyes fell upon a huge gray rock which stood
by the shore of the river. . . . And the rock was gray, and
ghastly, and tall, — and the rock was gray. . . .

"And I looked, . . . and there stood a man upon the summit of the rock. . . .

"And mine eyes fell upon the countenance of the man,
and his countenance was wan with terror. . . . And the man
shuddered, and turned his face away, and fled afar off, in haste,
so that I beheld him no more." — POE.

THIS is the story of the man who was
drowned at the Gray Rock of Abol. Here
is the whole story — all sides of it : make
of it what you will.

"The Indian thought that we should
lie by on Sunday," writes Thoreau, and it
is not the only instance where Thoreau
naïvely chronicles some attempt on the
part of Joe Polis to bring his manners up

to the standards of woods etiquette. " Said he, ' We come here lookum things, look all round; but come Sunday, lock up all that, and then Monday look again.' He spoke of an Indian of his acquaintance who had been with some ministers to Ktaadn, and had told him how they conducted. This he described in a low and solemn voice. ' They make a long prayer every morning and night, and at every meal. Come Sunday,' said he, ' they stop 'em, no go at all that day, — keep still, — preach all day, — first one, then another, just like church. Oh, ver good men.' "

Here evidently comes a gap in the conversation. It is plain that the hermit of Walden was not impressed by this improving example, or said something slighting, and Joe Polis, ever a stout debater, sought to strengthen his own argument for Sabbath-keeping by some unanswerable proof of the goodness of these men. Ordinarily, would Joe Polis have told the story that follows? He must have known many such, but he never told another to Thoreau. However, the proof of these men's piety being irrefutable, he brings it forth. "'One day,' said he, 'going along a river, they came to the body of a man in the water, drowned good while, all ready fall to pieces. They go right ashore, — stop there, go no farther that day, — they have meeting there, preach and pray just like Sunday. Then they get poles and lift up the body, and they go back and carry the body with them. Oh, they ver good men.'" Not a very correct account of what happened, as we shall see, but what Joe Polis thought he had heard from John Franceway,[1] who was there. The two Indians had agreed that to give Christian burial to this man was a sure proof of goodness.

But is the poet-naturalist impressed with the beauty of this act of piety to the unknown dead, the mere body of corruption now, but once a man, —

> " Cut off even in the blossoms of his sin,
> Unhousel'd, disappointed, unanel'd " ?

" I judged," said he, " from this account that their every camp was a camp-meeting,

[1] François, of course, but called Franceway when it was not made into Plassoway, Brassway, or Brassua.

and they had mistaken their route, — they should have gone to Eastham ; that they wanted an opportunity to preach more than to see Ktaadn. I read of a similar party that seem to have spent their time there singing the songs of Zion. I was glad that I did not go to that mountain with such slow coaches."

The reverse of the shield presents a very different picture.

The only one of this party whom I have known personally was, at the time of this little woods excursion in 1857, already something of a veteran in adventure. He had hunted big game on the coast of Africa and pirates in the China seas ; he had been harried and almost annihilated by such a typhoon as comes but twice in a century, and he was one of those who, with Commodore Perry, turned a leaf of destiny by ranging Japan with the nations of the West.[1]

By his friendly courtesy, I have under my hand an unpublished autograph ac-

[1] Professor John S. Sewall of the Bangor Theological Seminary.

count of this trip, written before Mr. Thoreau had ever set pen to paper upon his
own record. Such a vivacious little nar-
rative as it is, effervescing with puns and
bright word-play, turning all the hardships
of a toilsome cruise into the most laugh-
able of adventures. Not even Theodore
Winthrop's boyish account of his trip down
the West Branch touches the fun and frolic
of these psalm-singing ministers.

There were eighteen in the party, — ten
theological students, two friends of theirs,
and six boatmen, with three batteaus.
They made the trip from Bangor to the
top of Katahdin and back in ten days, coming from the summit of Katahdin into
Bangor in just three days, which must be
very near a record, there being no railroad
then above Oldtown. It was an uncommonly rainy year, and they suffered tor-
tures from black flies and mosquitoes. The
bulk of their food was hard-tack and dried
herring. They made forced marches, and
had totally insufficient tent-room. But
there is not the suspicion of a complaint
all through this little history, not even that

first night in a rainstorm, when eighteen men are trying to decide how they are all to sleep in a shelter tent but twenty feet long, and the problems of stowage are so great that one of the boatmen inquires whether "the long ones will take the tent lengthwise or crawl in twice." The meagreness of their outfit they made up for by the mock splendor of their titles, being officially known as the Grand Mufti, the Bivalvular Purveyor, the Drum Major, Esculapius, and the Bashaw of Two Tails, "who was no tale-bearer in spite of his slanderous title, whose duty it was to keep the stragglers up, to preserve the caudal extremity of the line in due proportions, and bring the tour at last to a successful termination." Upon the top of Katahdin the Grand Mufti fell to calculating "how large a constabulary would be required to put down such a rising of the mass," and the shivering Drum Major "broke out into demi-semi-quavers all over; in fact, his music only made to achieve alternately a 'shake' and a 'rest.'" Thus it is all, excellent fooling, not a bit like the "road to

Eastham." Mr. Thoreau need have had
no fears that he would not have been put
quite upon his mettle to keep up with either
the wit or the paces of this party.

In due place mention is made of that
Sunday spent in a camp of green boughs
just below the timber-line of Katahdin, —
" a Sabbath among the clouds, long to be
remembered as most like to the Sabbath
above the clouds. There were songs of
Zion — and meetings — even a sermon in
our gypsy camp. Had we climbed so far
toward heaven, yet not to get a glimpse of
the pearly gates? . . . Katahdin was to
us as were the Delectable Mountains to
Christian and Hopeful, whence could be
seen with telescopic faith some of the glory
of the Celestial City." (One has the right
to meditate upon what one wills; the curious may compare Mr. Thoreau's profitable
cogitations, when on the same spot, upon
Titans, Chaos, Vulcan, and Prometheus.)

Forty-seven years after that was written,
another member of the same party recalls
the day : —

" You remember the Sabbath we spent

upon Katahdin, the glorious outlook from the mountain, the serious, but grotesque appearance of our company as we joined in the Sabbath services, Parker in his shirt-sleeves and gloves, with mosquito netting over his head, preaching the sermon, while the rest of us, a number of whom have gone to worship in a grander temple, were reclining in positions which we would hardly commend to the congregations whom we have ministered to since in the House of God.

"One of my pleasantest memories of that Sabbath is of our boatmen, who seemed the most interested participants in that service, two of whom, I was told, not long after were converted and took a manly stand for Christ, one of them joining the church in Oldtown, and both dating the beginning of their religious interest from that Sabbath and the way we kept it, so different from any they had ever witnessed in that region. All of our party on that trip have seemed very near and dear to me, and not the least precious to my memory are the men who so kindly, and in such a brotherly way, guided and cared for us. How faithfully and nobly our Indian guide led us! Those rivermen are more serious and thoughtful than they usually have credit for. They are sharp and quick to read character, especially to know who is interested in them, and no men, I believe, are more faithful to a trust which has been committed to them in confidence."

The records are full, but upon one point there is not a word, and that is how they found and buried the body of that dead river-driver. Had not Thoreau recorded it, I, who have inquired somewhat closely into woods history and for many years have known the chronicler of the expedition, though hearing often enough of the man who was drowned at the Gray Rock of Abol, might never have heard the sequel to the story. The only public mention any of the twelve seems ever to have made of the incident was some time after Thoreau's thrust was published, when one of the party printed a brief statement of the facts in the "Congregationalist" for August 17, 1866. He says: —

"The body which we found near the head of Lake Pockwockamus was that of a poor lumberman, drowned some four or five weeks before, in driving logs. The spot was so near the ground where we had determined to halt for dinner, that we kept on, dined, and then a party of volunteers went back to perform the last rites of sepulture. A rudely carved fragment of slate was nailed to a tree at the head of the grave, and served to tell the occasional hunter in these trackless wilds of the disaster which had befallen the sleeper beneath. A brief prayer at the grave, with a few passages from the Book of Books, was the simple service which committed dust to dust.

"It was not because we were a party of 'slow coaches' that we halted for this act of respect to the remains of a brother man. The incident was certainly a sobering one; and yet there was a degree of satisfaction in being able to carry back to the friends the tidings that the body of him whom they mourned, and for whom they had twice sent parties in search, had been found and had received Christian burial."

These are the documents on both sides, for whose discrepancies in fact and feeling the two Indians, Polis and Franceway, are accountable. They are more than the mere papers in a case. Here, on either side, drawn up as if in review, are the two parties to the difference, men with the best that culture, learning, and philosophy could give, yet neither seeing in the incident anything deeply significant; and between them files this little column of woods-bred men who read in it so· much more, who are so struck by its rarity and beauty that they listen gladly to sermons and change the current of their lives. They speak of it to each other and, as it flies, the story grows until what seems truth to Joseph Polis is quite unlike the facts.

Deep impressions imply adequate causes: what was sufficient so to impress Joe Polis? For he did not get his version of the story from John Franceway. John knew that only a part of his company went back to bury this man. The chronicler, cross-examined, says that he was washing dishes for eighteen men; others also were absent. John knew that they made no unnecessary delay, for on that day, the twenty-sixth of June, they covered the whole distance from the foot of Ambajejus Carry to the mouth of Abol Stream. Doubtless he told Joe Polis this, and Joe, knowing the country well, could not forget it. Only twenty-four days elapsed between the date of John Franceway's return and the day upon which Thoreau wrote in his journal, not time enough for a woodsman to forget anything which had been told him; yet here is Joseph Polis, fully convinced of its truth, telling Thoreau, "in a low and solemn voice," that the whole party stopped a full half day on Pockwockamus Carry, about midway of their actual day's journey, in order to do honor to the grave of an unknown man, and the implication is strong that the most of this time was filled with religious services on his behalf. No wonder that to Thoreau it touched on the grotesque!

How is this to be accounted for? Fraud it is not; it cannot be forgetfulness; lack of information is hardly possible; it can-

not be from a pious reverence for masses
for the dead — for Joe Polis was a Pro-
testant Indian.[1] It is sheer artistic instinct,
the human trait of wishing to inclose what
is uniquely excellent in the rarest and cost-
liest setting. Joseph Polis had improved
the story unconsciously.

Thoreau, who had come into the Maine
woods to study the Indian, might well
have taken time to probe this subtle matter, for here is something truly strange.
However, with his luckless knack of
blundering when he came in contact with
men, in his own phrase, he "improved his
opportunity to be ignorant." The most
significant incident that ever came under
his observation while he was in the Maine
woods he bungled utterly. Once, indeed,
he had been hot on the trail of a solution.
In camp at Kineo he had seen for the first
time a bit of phosphorescent wood, and
kindled by its cold fire, he writes four
pages about the phenomenon. " It suggested to me that there was something to
be seen if one had eyes. It made a be-

[1] So he told Thoreau ; but he died a Catholic.

liever of me more than before. I believed
that the woods were not tenantless, but
choke-full of honest spirits as good as myself any day." [1] But in just two days from
that time Thoreau was shutting the mouth
of the man who could have told him all
he wanted to know. Joe Polis knew all
about the man who was drowned on the
Gray Rock of Abol; Joe Polis could have
shown him all the spirits he wanted to
see!

Ah, the graves in the woods that one
who knows can tell of, lying singly, by
twos, by threes, by half-dozens! This
One, That One, The Other, — then, as
recollection must travel back of the limits
of one man's life, Some One, Nobody-
Knows-Who, but it must have been a
grave, for the ground is springy and hol-
lowed, and about there is a line of mould
as if long back a fence of logs had guarded
a little space. So many of them! and
every one doomed to be obliterated within

[1] Pp. 244–248, *Maine Woods*, New Riverside Edition.
The context is well worth looking up.

the lifetime of the men who knew all about them. That is what gets upon a man's mind and gnaws it like a bone, the knowing that where he falls he will lie, like a log in the forest, unburied or lost to recollection. The quiet cemetery with white palings and neat headstones; the narrow, orderly streets; the heaped-up mounds grown with grass; the society of kindred and acquaintance although in perpetual silence, and the undisturbed possession of even a narrow plot of earth come to him in his visions with a desire as strong as the longing for life itself. He knows how it will be with him, — to be jammed in the rapids under rocks, to float in some dark eddy, to be cast out under the tossing, creaking flowage of some lake, never to be found, or to be buried by the pathway, even so near that the passing will soon go on over his head, and the men who come after and curse the hollow in the road that fills up with water will not know that it is his grave. It was so with those three buried at Howe Falls on Nahmakanta, where supplies were hauled over the graves on purpose that the men might not know and lose their courage. He remembers at Pollywog Pond the eight graves in one place, and one in another, of those drowned on Nigger Pitch; two at the mouth of Bean Brook ; seven at Howe Falls Deadwater, of those who died of smallpox, and six more at Logan Joe Mary, dead of the same scourge. There are all those who have died at Ripogenus, and those down by Grand Falls, where their names are scratched upon the rocks, the only enduring memorial in all the woods. How many he knows of here and there, lying singly, unmarked, buried in silence to wait in awful solitude. Every grave is his own in possibility : he never thinks of it slightingly. Death is still Death in the woods, though outside now it may be nothing but death.

Yet not even the solemnity of a death in the wilderness explains why John Franceway and those other five, some of whom knew this man and were near at hand when he was drowned, regarded this incident as so deeply solemn. For it was not the prayers and preaching upon the mountain, it was something else that so impressed them. Behind the stage on which they were but players was the terrifying hell-fire of Calvinism, Methodism, Wesleyanism, mingling in contiguous incongruity with the Romanist's purging flames; and before that lurid background they were all playing in a drama of redemption and damnation, not knowing when any one of them was to leave the stage, nor what he was ordained to do upon it. But this man's part was clear: he had played it out to damnation, and made his exit, and no man might deny that the doom was warrantable. It was the tragic rightness of his fate, than which the greatest of the playwrights have conceived nothing more sternly just, that conquered their imaginations.

For they knew the whole story; they had witnessed the man's sin and his prompt, almost miraculous punishment; and they knew that his ghost cried unburied; yet now they saw him redeemed from the damned into purgatorial hope, and, by a special providence of God, given what no

man buried in those woods had ever had
before, the rites of Christian sepulture, —
a man who died under the curse of God,
by a just judgment; who was lost irrecoverably; who was found at the last possible moment, his grave consecrated, his
spirit set at rest.

Moreover, because the Indian who saw
it chanced to tell another within three
weeks of his return, and because that one
by a still rarer chance told it to a man who
wrote everything down, even the things he
did not understand, the man who died forsaken and alone has had the whole world
come to his obsequies. So far from being
placed obscurely in the wilderness, that
Gray Rock of Abol stands in the eyes and
sight of all.

These are strange stories, but they well
up out of the hearts of men, and in them
are the issues of life. Men do not perish
alone, unknown, forsaken, forgotten. The
constitution of the universe forbids. The
truth about them must leap out some time,
and be written on the skies like the flashes
of the midnight Aurora; somewhere it is

to be known what they were, where they failed, wherein they made their conquests, — their treachery, their faithfulness — their cowardice, their courage — their shameless- ness, their honor — but most of all and longest enduring, their better parts.

We come now to the story, no more the facts about the story, but the story itself.

There are many gray rocks on Abol: Mount Katahdin put them there. Ka- tahdin rules over all that West Branch country, a calm despot. Mute, massive, immense, hard-featured, broad-shouldered, nowhere can you get in that country where the broad forehead of Katahdin is not turned upon you. Snow and rain it sends to that region; it floods the river from its flanks; its back cuts off the north wind, making the valley hot; the road of the farmer it has closed, and the way of the lumberman it makes unduly difficult, by sowing the whole country with millions of tons of granite chipped from its sides. From Abol all

the way down those many falls, Pockwockamus, Katepskonhegan, called more often
Debsconeag, Pescongamoc, which we now
call Passangamet, and Ambajejus, the river
in half a dozen places is choked with these
great granite boulders, quarried by the frost
from the sides of Katahdin, and by the ice
transported all over the country. Katahdin makes all that region what it is; it
made the falls, and, indirectly, the back-
breaking carries around them; it made
the sand on Abol, the first place on the way
downstream where you notice clear sand
above freshet level; it turned the course
of the glaciers and so directed the horsebacks of the glacial drift; it made the Norway pines [1] that grow on the horsebacks,
with their hearse-like plumes switching in
the breeze like stiff, rustling silk; and it
made all the gray rocks. In this region
a " gray rock," or a " great gray," is the
accepted synonym for a boulder of Katahdin granite.

Abol is the first fall upon which Katah-

[1] *Pinus resinosa*, the red pine, " wrongly called Norway pine," says Gray, but here always so misnamed.

din has laid a heavy finger,[1] being the nearest to the mountain. It goes by many names, according as the Indian has been twisted into forms more or less easy for the lumberman's tongue, — Aboljecarme-*gus*cook, Abolje*car*megus, Aboljackne*ge*-sic, Aboljacko*me*gus, Aboljackarne*gas*sic, — but it means just the same to say simply Abol. The signification is not "smooth ledge falls," as Thoreau gives it — that is Sowadabscook, a hundred miles farther down. The name means " place where the water laughs in coming down," and belongs to two streams of crystal water, blue as ice, that spring from the side of Katahdin and enter the river just above the falls, which by Indian custom take their name from the stream.

The fall at Abol is nothing stupendous. There is half a mile of very rough water, but no sharp pitch. At the head, on the right, lies a low, sandy island overgrown

[1] Not to be construed as meaning that there is no granite above this point. Loose granite appears on the lower end of Ripogenus, and ledge granite not far below, but the drift boulders are not aggressively conspicuous till near to Abol.

with inferior brushwood, and, like the rest of the carry, bearing a few scattered Norway pines. The passage behind it is closed by a wing dam, making a dry way; one might go upon the island without thinking that it had ever been parted from the shore.

Here by the head of the island are the gray rocks of Abol. They lie close to the water, at some stages under it, great slabs of granite, as true as if split out by the hand of man. Most of them are from fifteen to eighteen feet long, about four and a half feet deep, and of a thickness varying from that of a thin slab of nine or ten inches to one of two and a half feet mean width. Several lie parallel, their fractures curving coincidently, showing that they have been split since they arrived. All are large, but one ranks all the others. It is thirty-six and a half feet long, five feet and ten inches at its widest point, and four feet and nine inches at its greatest thickness, with mean dimensions not very considerably less, perfect in shape, the most tremendous natural obelisk anywhere to be found. These are the gray rocks of Abol, rifted out of the side of old Katahdin, which crouches lion-like only six miles off, watching them as the Sphinx watches the little shrine between his paws, looking out over the desolation of the wilderness.

When the water is at its height, most of these slabs are submerged, but there is one rock that is always above the surface. This is the one that has a name. Old men sometimes call it the Goodwin Rock, but those who are younger and those who came before, for fifty, sixty, perhaps almost a hundred years, have known it as the Gray Rock of Abol. Standing where it does, within the suck of the current, though so near inshore, — for the current draws upon the head of the island, — a man is always stationed upon it when the logs are running, to prevent jams from forming. There is not the slightest danger in working upon the Gray Rock. It is about three feet out of water at driving-pitch, dry always; it is close inshore; the water is not yet rough, only strong; and it is the coarse granite from Katahdin, upon which a man's foot cannot slip. There is no danger at all upon the Gray Rock, no more than upon a ball-room floor.

But now it is almost fifty years since Goodwin of Stetson found that rock his doom. Of a May morning, too, when the little wintergreen sprouts, tender and red, were coming up on the cradle-knolls, and the bees were in the blueberry blooms, and here and there a wild woods-straw-berry, blossoming white, made the drivers think of home. There was such a bright stillness on the morning, and Katahdin, the old giant, still snow-capped, looked down benignly, as if he had waked up good-natured, and, throwing off his blan-ket of clouds, had put up his head before doffing his nightcap. " Good-morning to you ! " he called out to the river-drivers working on the foaming river a full mile below his crown. They waved him back a salute. They yelled as they worked. It was great fun to work on such a clean, crisp morning, and as they felt the strength of the current and rode down to the head of the falls, balancing on a single log, they yelled at Goodwin on the Gray Rock.

That was not Goodwin's day to be merry. Something had gone wrong with him, and he stood on that gray granite from the mist-time of early morning till luncheon-time, when they lost him, a sombre figure wrapped in sullen thoughts, lunging spitefully with his pick-pole at every log, however innocent of evil intentions of jamming, that ran out a blunt nose by his rock just to have a look at him. Whenever they came near him, the poor dumb logs, he prodded them viciously with his pick-pole, and drove them off into the slick of the current and cursed them for their stupidity. Not even the brightness of the morning beguiled him from his evil humor. No man knew what the matter was. He did not have a bad name, his mates spoke well of him; it might have been homesickness; it might have been the toothache; it might have been the wave of world-woe that surges over a man now and then from depths he cannot sound; but there he stood, all alone on the gray granite, stretching out his fist in wanton perversity of spirit, and with blackening oaths cursed God Almighty, damning God to God's own face in the wilderness all alone.

" There ain't no sense in talkin' that way," said one man to another in disapproval as they rode down past on their logs.

" It's darin' *too* much, even in a safe place like he's in, it is," replied the other, riding his log right into the white of the rapid; " I wouldn't do it, not here, not for no money."

Still the man on the shore station cursed, swore, damned with imprecations everything that came near him, and no one knew, no one ever knew, what was the trouble with him.

For he disappeared. He was in a safe place, and he fell off. He was in quiet water, strong, not bad, and he did not reach the shore. He was a good swimmer, but he never struck out. One man saw above the slope of the current downstream of the rock, a pair of hands reaching up toward heaven, — just a pair of hands, never anything more.

The man who had seen this told the others. "I seen him stand there like he was on a barn floor, and I seen him lift up his fist an' shake it right stret in the face of old Katahdin, an' I hearn him holler like his voice would rattle lead inside him, 'To hell with God!' An' then when I looked the Gray Rock was all empty, an' in the water I seen only his two sets of fingers movin' slow-like in the mist that sticks close to the black slick of the falls. I seen 'em open once, an' then they shut an' was gone."

"That was a judgment," said the men one to another.

"That was sure a judgment for swearin'," they answered solemnly, continuing their search for his body.

But the body was not to be found.

"And it ain't to be expected it ever will be. It ain't often that you do find 'em when they dies so by a judgment," said one of the wise ones who could remember much that had happened on the river. "Lucky for you fellows if everything keeps quiet around here. I'm glad I'm goin' right

along with the head of the drive and shan't
have to camp none on *this* carry."

The man next to him — who was to
stay — looked at him a little startled —
and kept silent.

It was as they had predicted, nothing
was ever found of the man, though two
parties were sent up on purpose to search
after the drive had passed down. " He left
a mother," as the phrase is, which means
in woods talk that he was the only son of
a widow, and for his mother's sake all was
done that could be. But the search was
fruitless.

" I knew it would be just that way,"
said the wise one; " it 's *always* so with
judgments; that 's a part of it — they can't
never be quiet till they are buried, and
they don't never get buried, not that kind,
when they die damning God that way."

What of the weeks that followed in the
desolation of the wilderness? The little
flowers sprouted leaves and buds, and the
buds grew to blossoms; the pine pollen
drifted down in golden showers, and the

tree swallow built her nest. Everything alive was happy and moving. There was no foot of man, however, on those carries. Showers fell and the damp they left dried up, and never a human foot-track was imprinted upon the softened soil. But round about the rocks of Abol, under the pines on the carry, those tall and funereal Norways, what was it that wailed and cried?

" Crushed by the waves upon the crag was I,
    Who still must hear these waves among the dead,
  Breaking and brawling on the promontory,
    Sleepless ; and sleepless is my weary head!
.   .   .   .
  Nor Death that lulleth all, can lull my ghost,
    One sleepless soul among the souls that sleep!"

" And I would n't not want to camp on that carry, not now," says the hunter; " for mebbe I should be for seein' things."

Your guide is not superstitious. Ask him if he believes in ghosts, and he will look straight through and beyond you. "No," says he, as short and sharp as a rifle-crack.

But then your guide knows many things

which it is not to be expected that he will impart to you. When the wind sobs outside and the rain is on the roof, the fall rain that brings down the withered leaves, and you sit by the fire listening to the wailing wind, then will be the time you choose to talk to him of things you know yourself. It was your father's cousin who had warning when his friend's ship went down in the China seas; the day and the hour he knew. Did his friend not appear at his bedside at the edge of dawn, his hat crushed down over his eyes and a gray ship's blanket drawn around his shoulders, just as he had sprung up the companion-way when the ship reeled under her last blow and foundered? It was two days after they had cleared from Hong Kong, and he always knew what he saw. Your uncle, he had seen things too. Once, when he was sitting in his cabin in mid-ocean, in the calm of evening, a woman passed through the room wringing her hands, and she passed through again and wrung her hands, and a third time, still wringing her hands, and he never knew what it meant, only he saw it.

"And it's lucky he didn't ask her no questions," says the guide, speaking up promptly; "for any one that talks to a ghost, they don't live the year out, they don't live long mostly. I knowed a man — and it was my father — he was follered by a ghost, and she spoke. She asked him for a cup of salt he had borrered, and he said he'd pay it back, and he did, but he didn't live long after that."

Your guide is not superstitious, but he has seen some strange things. He knows, for one, that murdered men and suicides and men who have died under a judgment are never easy till something is done for them. "If a man kills himself, his ghost is bound to stay around the place he did it's long's the house is there; there was Frank Black killed himself in a camp up by Grant Farm, year the war broke out, and they didn't have no peace nor quiet long as them camps stayed. And if a man is murdered, he will stay round till his body is found; if you want to know for sure, there's the way Dudley Maxfield's ghost ha'nts round that poke-logan hole up to

Ayers's Rips. But if a man dies under a judgment, then they don't never find his body, not at all, and that was how it was with Larry Connors."

Up and down that carry at Abol all that month and the next ranged the spirit of the man who was drowned at the Gray Rock. That is the name he has come to be known by, not his own, but as "the man who was drowned at the Gray Rock of Abol."

In the rain beneath the Norways, in the moonlight by the sandy carry-end, he paced till cock-crow. The nights were short then, but he paced till daybreak. In the cloud of the falls-mist he wandered, more impalpable than that, searching among the rocks for his former habitation. When he had found it, down along the tangled shores of the deadwater below Abol, he traveled, slowly, each night a trifling journey, following what he must not lose sight of, desiring infinitely the burial which was to be denied him.

"To have no peace in the grave, is that not sad?"

Shorter still grew the nights, yet longer

grew his journeyings, for the stream became stronger and talked louder, and threw
up spray and beat among the rocks of the
ragged Pockwockamus. It is a rough and
terrible journey down among those rocks,
and the lost soul might well have shuddered as he saw what happened to the
tenantless and battered body, useless, yet
still so precious, which he was following.
On the shortest night of the year, it came
safely out of the current of the deadwater
into an eddy some distance below the fall.

It was, and doubtless still is, a pretty
spot, with tall trees overarching and a
sandy shore, so quiet and beautiful, and
yet not far above are the great gray rocks
and the thunder of the falls. There by the
moonlight, upon the sandy shore, all night
long and many nights paced the tortured
spirit. The current does not move that
eddy, — and the sun beats down upon it,
— and the days of grace are numbered,
— and no one comes.

Then the woods resound with singing.
All up and down the river the shores

reverberate, and Katahdin smiles grimly, his head bare and bald now to the summer sun, to see the joyous troop that comes along. What jokes they make, what merriment on the hot, hard carries, what a pace they travel at! The woods at that day had never seen such a throng of pleasure-seekers. Eighteen men of them, and all singing!

But the guides were thoughtful at times, and sometimes they looked at one another or passed a quiet word. It had begun at Ambajejus that morning, when one boatman slyly nudged another and asked privately, "Where 'll we be campin' down to-night?"

"Head of Pockwockamus most likely," was the answer. "It's a strong pull from there to the top of the mountain in one day, but seein' they want to camp on top, that's the easiest thing to do. We'd better save our backs on these carries what we can to-day, and take it out of our legs to-morrow."

"You can count me out on that Pockwockamus bough-down," said the first, and he made a pretext of looking at the pitch on the boats to draw the other away with him out of ear-shot of the rest. "Think a minit," he said; "where do you s'pect that that Gooding has got to? You can just bet your money that it's no bone to camp downstream of *him*."

"It ought to be all right with ten ministers along to keep the boogers off," demurred the first; "and it's too hard a trip to try to make all these carries in one day, with three boats and only six of us fit to lug boat. It's two miles of solid carry, and that makes 'most six miles of lugging boat, too much for one day, and it's most as hard poling up over them rocky hell-holes; and then that dratted old mountain to-morrow. Tell you, flesh and blood has some rights, I guess, as well as dead folks!"

"You'll find *me* campin' just upstream of Abol when you come to hunt me up to-mor' mornin'," said the first quietly.

"Oh, they don't do folks no hurt that ever I heerd of," remarked the other.

"Well, I seen him alive mebbe last of

any one, and I ain't a-goin' to take no risks. I ain't lost no ghosts, an' I don't want nobody's else's huntin' me up an' bein' sociable. What's to hender droppin' some of our boats along? We can leave the little wangan-boat right here at the foot of Ambajejus, and drop one of the big ones at the foot of Pockwockamus, and let them fellers farm it from there up. That makes only one boat on the last two carries, an' two on Debsconeag an' this, and saves a whole barrel of backaches. Tip the wink to John an' we 'll do it."

"Think them fellers will suspicion anything?" asked the other.

"Them?" retorted the other. "They 'll be blind as bats that has lost their spettacles; lots of things left for *them* to l'arn arter they get 'em all booked up down to the Institootion! This ain't no place for us to be stoppin' to eddicate *them*, 'less we show 'em how to ride shank's mare on these blasted carries."

The plan was adopted; the boatmen breathed more freely. It was just at dinner-time, a quarter of a mile below the foot of

Pockwockamus Carry, where the beach is
sandy and the water shoals inshore, that
they came upon the body of the man who
for five weeks had been missing.

There they gave him Christian burial,
close by the water, very close, as it had
to be, and yet above the line of the fresh-
ets. "Two of our boatmen knew him,"
writes he who headed the burial party,[1]
"and spoke very kindly and feelingly
of him. The body was much swollen, and
so decomposed that we could only dig a
shallow grave in the sand close beside it,
which the boatmen made with their paddles. The men gently and reverently lifted
the body into its resting-place; we had a
funeral service; one of the men covered
the remains with sheets of birch bark
which he cut from a tree, and we all seemed
to be brothers united by more than any
earthly tie, as we proceeded on in our
journey."

For the first time ever known within
these woods, a man had received Christian
burial.

[1] The Rev. F. P. Chapin of Hudson, N. H.

The boatmen did not talk much about it then. It was not till they were camped by the mouth of the lower Abol, the fire blazing and supper eaten, that two of them, by a common inclination, wandered off to the shore of the clear stream and sat there in the sunset afterglow, which turned Katahdin to a purple amethyst and flushed the water pink beyond the dark reflection of the further bank.

They sat silent. One had a bit of hardtack, and he crumbled it slowly to toss to the fishes, watching the lunges that the white chevin, ever active at twilight, made for the flakes as they settled.

"Them 's awful spry fish, them chubs," said he, as if natural history were all that weighed upon his mind; "I 've seen 'em 'fore now peel a raw potato all white just jumpin' at it that way, s' sharp in their jaws. And the' 's eels, too, they 're all for — they 're *bad*," said he, suddenly checking himself. "You seen how it was to-day? *You* understood?"

The other shook his shoulders, but did not reply.

The one who found a relief in words went on. " One minister is enough to do the job for most of us; he ought n't to be so very bad off with *ten* of 'em — think so ? "

" Guess he *needed* most of 'em," responded the other, not too hopeful.

" But don't ye think that 'mongst 'em they could menege to git him his 'Come-all-yer'? " It was a free woods rendering of the Scripture invitation, " Come unto me, all ye that labor, and are heavy laden, and I will give you rest."

"Well," he went on, not insisting on an answer, " it was an awful lucky thing for him that they chanceted to come along just now, for he could n't have fleeted much longer. No one can't say that Friday wa'n't no lucky day for him."

The other did not speak. The silence suited him. He sat with his hands around his knees, looking at the red glow of the evening sky and the twinkling evening star. " Say," said he at length, " how hot do you s'pose hell is anyhow? "

The next day was Saturday and they

climbed the mountain. By the next this man was ripe to listen to sermons, and it is reported that they did him no harm.

The next day they all came flying down and pushed far along on their road to the settlements. On the way they paused. It was by the grave of the man whom they had buried. One of them — it was Chapin, who had headed the burial party — brought forth a piece of slate that he had with him and nailed it to the tree at the head of the grave. It said only : —

George Goodwin, June 26, 1857.

More they did not know, neither age, nor home, nor the day he died.

It was almost certainly Sunday labor by which that rude inscription was scratched with a jack-knife upon the bit of slate, — found upon the granite side of Katahdin where slate is rare, and carefully treasured under many difficulties against this use, — but it was labor to be justified by the strictest Pharisee. Never again would they have opportunity to mark that lonely grave with any sign that it was consecrated ground. So they nailed it to the tree at the head of the sleeper, who did not stir, nor moan, nor attempt to talk to them, and they left him there to sleep until the Judgment.

Tree and tablet are both gone now, I am told ; a simple post marks the place, just opposite the head of the second island in Pockwockamus Deadwater, on the right shore, directly across from Ben Harris's camp. An Indian guide tells me that he now and then clears out about it to keep the forest from encroaching, and after his day some one else will take up the task. It is consecrated ground, the only hallowed spot in all that limitless forest. There, two rods from the water, three at most, close by the place where they found him, still rest the bones of the man who was drowned on the Gray Rock of Abol and, by a miracle of God, after death found mercy.

VI

A CLUMP OF POSIES

A CLUMP OF POSIES

I never met the lady face to face, and none of the men ever told me whether they thought her plain or pretty, though they gave out that she was "all right," and that they were *Amici usque ad aras*, or its woods equivalent. However, there can be no question about the truth of the story : for we were in the woods that year and had the same guide, Wilbur Webster, who was drowned that winter in the lake behind Kineo. Were he alive, he would vouch for all I say ; but I heard enough of it from others. On the whole it is a pretty story.

Down on Ripogenus, where the little knoll springs in the road to give you a view over the treetops of that rounded mountain with the shining patches of ledge near its summit, from which all hunters long have called it the Squaw's Bosom, — just about halfway across the carry, a natural resting-place, and delightful withal because it is so cosy and yet so open, is the Putting-in Place, where in spring the river-drivers launch their boats for the adventurous passage of the other mile and a half of Ripogenus. It is delightful there in springtime, hedged with birches, carpeted with bracken, murmuring with the hum of bees and of the rushing river many rods below.

There the batteaus are laid out bottom up; there the fire smokes under the searing-irons and the keg of pitch is kept hot, while the old batteau-pitcher, deft and wise at his trade, goes over the sides and bottom of each one, and daubs and smears and sears with his irons until he has made ready each boat for her ordeal by water, soon to be undergone. Here he sings to himself and smokes, runs his left hand lightly but searchingly over the smooth surface, scanning it with close-bent head, before he lifts himself with hands on hips to straighten his bowed back. He is an old man, used to the River; he likes his calling, but he does not meddle much with young and little

things, either to notice or to molest. ·The
brown hare thumps up and sniffs at him
and thumps off again ; the vireos and red-
starts carol to him without his hearing; and
the little flowers grow bravely, unpicked
and perhaps unseen. Even the coy lady's-
slipper,[1] that wanton, wayward flower, who
spreads her skirts and flutters her ribbons,
curtsying and coquetting, playing fast-and-
loose with all her lovers; who hides herself
in the forest and turns invisible and every
year seeks a new home, — even she did
not try to fascinate the old man by her
capriciousness, but grew boldly out in the
sunshine, in a great clump, as thickset as a
garden plant, and almost within the cart-
track of the carry road. These, however,
were the demurest little flowers, not blush-
ing pinkish like their coquettish sisters, but
immaculately white and as staid as Quaker-
esses ; they raised their eleven little heads
— a very large family for their tribe — and
lifted their great waxen lips and spread
their fluttering pennons in purest inno-

[1] *Cypripedium acaule*, the stemless lady's-slipper, our
only common species here.

cence and childlikeness. There was never a prettier bunch of lady's-slippers, and yet of the almost two hundred men who passed there several times a day, not one seemed to have any more eyes than the old batteau-pitcher, not one had ever given them the compliment of a glance. It took something very like a miracle to make those men see what one would have supposed that they could not help seeing; for the little clump of posies is the beginning and the middle and the ending of this story.

A miracle is, literally, something which excites astonishment. The cause may be decried as commonplace, but there was certainly no deficiency in the effect when the men came dragging in at dusk from their outposts to the camp at the upper end of Ripogenus, and found a new tent there pitched right among their own, and in it a Woman.

"Well, that does beat all hell!" was their frank comment, and there followed interrogations very much to the point, in satisfaction of which those who were lucky

enough to have been at the upper end
of the carry that afternoon, and therefore
possessed of the news, announced that
though she wa'n't quite a pullet, she wa'n't
no old hen neither.

"Schoolma'am?"

"Naw! Not a bittee!"

"Glasses an' short hair?"

"Naw!" (more viciously). "All right,
I tell ye, all right, an' Wilbur Webster
backs the deal. Friends of Joe Francis's
an' Steve's, an' come up the Lake[1] with the
Old Man, who's comin' down to-morrer.
Stands to the West Branch Drive to do
the pretty thing by 'em."

Up in the carpenter shop, which was
built on an extravagant scale, with the sky
for a roof and the whole earth for a floor,
and nothing else in it but a litter of shav-
ings and a tall horse for making poles and
peavey handles, some of the older men
discussed the incident without approval.

The grumbler, who was not young,
swore about the folly of bringing a woman
on the drive where men had to work and

[1] "The Lake" always meant Moosehead.

did n't want to be side-stepping, and where they mebbe might like to talk some to their blame selves all on the quiet when the blank logs was contrairy, 'thout havin' to stop and think who was by.

One of the others suggested that at the worst she could n't be everywhere to once, — which was axiomatic, — and as there was a hunderd an' seventy-five of them against her alone, they could gamble on at least a hunderd and seventy-four chances in their favor, which was long odds.

Still the grumbler allowed that it was rank inconsiderate to come their way at all ; that the drive wa'n't no place for a woman anyways, and folks that knowed when they was well off stayed to home and let men work ; and if the women took to comin' there so thick, they'd be just 'bliged to leave the logs in the woods to rot all by their blank selves. He was right, too. Tourists have no more business on the drive than Sunday-school picnics have between firing-lines, and if anything unpleasant happens, they may blame themselves.

There was no rejoicing among the old men over the advent of a woman. Down the hill, in the two long rows of open-fronted tents, with the fires between, the younger fellows also sat in gloom. It did seem a little homey, perhaps, to have a girl around, especially to know that there was a *nice* girl around, whom one could look at without speaking to, and who would be as much above the reek of their daily life as if living on the top of Katahdin. (She had on a red dress? Well, just like a red-bird in a glass case, to be looked at respectfully without touching.) Ripogenus was hard enough to get logs and boats over; and the life was monotonous in spite of its dangers. This would be something different, something like going to church, thought one or two. Maybe she might speak to some of them, to a few of them, to one or two of them anyway.

Then they looked across the fire at the fellows on the other side of it. And they saw themselves! Such a set of tatterde-malions never graced a corn-field. They looked from man to man and saw hardly a whole garment apiece. They saw rags, and they saw holes, and they saw scriptural patches of new cloth upon old garments, producing the prophesied rents. There were men with trousers abbreviated to a sort of trunks, or cut off just below the knee to prevent " calking," and some sensitive souls, who abhorred setness of design, wore their nether garments with one leg cut below and the other above the knee. There were some without coat, vest, or trousers, or any part of them, but attired in full suits of underwear. This economical and attractive costume, sometimes white, but oftener originally a vivid scarlet, reduced by rains and perspiration to a whitish red, once whole perhaps, but now pinned together with huge horse safety-pins and variously adorned with patches of old mittens, was an ultra style which would have attracted attention in the most exclusive circles. There were men in rigs in which they would not have let their own mothers see them, and men who, tired and hungry as they were, would not have come down the carry-path till after dark, had they known beforehand that there was a woman on the carry. Oh, the dove-cote of the West Branch Drive got fluttered that time!

But what cause had they to look for such a calamity? It was thunder out of a clear sky, — everything all right in the morning when they left, and then the thunderbolt! No human foresight could have warded off the stroke, for never within the memory of the oldest man, not of the log-marker, nor the carpenter, nor the batteau-pitcher, not of the men who had almost outlived their usefulness, had there ever been a woman on the drive.

" And to have my broadcloth suit to home!" lamented one of the most out at elbows, breaking the gloom.

" And that Chinyman ain't sent back my shiny collars yet this week," said another, the joke being that there was not a Celestial within a hundred miles as the crow flew, nor a starched collar within two days' woods journey.

" Well, you 'd ort to see me in my pay-tent leathers and high dickey and ram-beaver," put in a third; "I reckon I'm just scrum when I *do* get fixed up; but it hain't no use; this here toney underwear that I'm a-sportin' is too far ahead o' the spring styles for this northern climate; makes me look like a last year's bird's nest."

"I count a old swamp robin's nest[1] a heap tidier lookin' set o' tatters 'n them clo'es what you have on, Bill. It don't look quite so all fallin' to pieces; but the wangan bills on this drive 's goin' to be somethin' hijjus. I was hopesin' to come out with a dollar or two to the good, time we got into boom, but I guess I sh'll blow it all in for wangan, and come out in the Comp'ny's debt same 's ush'al."

The man next to him was looking at his feet stretched out to the fire. There were neither heels nor toes to the socks he had on, but still he accounted them presentable; anything is that has an inch or two of the top left.

[1] "Swamp robin" is the vernacular name for the hermit thrush and also for the olive-backed, the two not being distinguished by woodsmen; but as the former nests on the ground, this man must have meant the olive-backed thrush's or even the catbird's nest.

" Guess I sh'll hev to give 'em their time, boys; they 'll do for patches anyhow. If there was more pairs of 'em, it would be easier to shingle 'em on over the wust o' the holes. Say, can't I swap my jack-knife for a pair of old mittens ? "

Thereupon the price of old mittens and stockings went up by jumps, till the market in worn-out socks was the firmest ever known on the drive. No danger of its being suddenly beared by some one with a reserve of foot and hand gear. That year there was n't a cast-off garment left upon the end of the carry, and every one knows that usually the path of the drive is littered with old clothes and old shoes. The demand for thread and needles was lively also, and had any one been playing Peeping Polly that night, long after their usual hour for turning in, the West Branch Drive might have been seen bending over their work, patching by firelight, in weariness of soul, but with the honest intention of being presentable on the morrow.

But when they got a chance at the wangan chest and could endow themselves in its glories, what a brave array of aniline they did present! Even Solomon might have studied their attire to the profitable neglect of the lily of the field. To attempt to describe the styles at Ripogenus that year would beggar the describer. Full suits of underwear went out of fashion with a bound, and a kaleidoscope of cut and color followed, — red, blue, green, yellow, stripes, plaids, patches. The Girl had known a little of the rainbow attractions of Epstein's and of Pretto's, but such cheerful combinations of color were wholly new; she wondered where is the Zeitgeist's shop and the roaring loom which wove such clothes. Some no doubt they brought into the woods with them; some they purchased from the wangan chest; but some must have come straight from Tom a Bedlam's. It would have turned the head of any girl who thought that so much was done on her account. This one never dreamed of that, — I have thought since then that she was rather stupid, for a girl. She was pleased with the fantastic costumes and with their picturesqueness

against the green background, she found
O'Connor a good comrade, and she forgot that she was either part of the show
herself — or the sole spectator. Least of
all did she imagine that she and the gentlemen of the extraordinary clothes were
taking parts in a little comedy of courtesy,
chivalry, and sentiment as pretty as it was
light. Something of it she perceived while
she was with them; a part she did not
learn till after she had left them; and the
prettiest part of all she would never have
known anything about, had not the clump
of posies at the Putting-in Place stopped
her to tell a dolorous tale.

When the Girl went up to visit O'Connor on the drive, it was in the face of
some friendly expostulation. O'Connor is
known to be a noisy lad, and quiet folk
are sometimes aghast at his perform-
ances.

" You could hear him when he started from the Rapo-
    genus Chutes,
You could hear the cronching-cranching of his swashing,
    spike-sole boots,

You could even hear the colors in the flannel shirt he
     wore,
And the forest fairly shivered at the way O'Connor
     swore.
'T was averred that in the city, full a hundred miles
     away,
They felt a little tremor when O'Connor drew his pay.

. . . .

" O'Connor reached the city and he reached it with
     a jar,
He had piled up all the cushions in the centre of the
     car.
— Had set them all on fire, and around the blazing
     pile
He was dancing 'dingle breakdowns' in a very jovial
     style.
And before they got him cornered they had rung in
     three alarms,
And it took the whole department to tie his legs and
     arms." [1]

Of course the drive is not all O'Connor;
no one estimates, at the highest figure, that
it will yield more than nine hundred and
twenty-five one thousandths pure O'Connor, the remainder being an alloy of the
virtues. Even Bangor is philistine to this

[1] "O'Connor from the Drive," in Mr. Holman F.
Day's *Pine Tree Ballads*.

extent; for the wisdom of Bangor about woodsmen is largely the fruit plucked from the tree of police-court knowledge. So Bangor had said, and said seriously : "Why do you take your daughter up there? How *dare* you do it — among all those rough men? Do you really think it is — ?" But he thought it *was*. Bangor does not realize that, next to his courage, what most distinguishes O'Connor is his respectful behavior to women. He may be drunk, but he is never insolent to a lady, never affronts her by look or comment, never makes it unpleasant for her to pass through the streets that he frequents.

When in the woods and lacking all the temptations which make city life so briefly but uproariously happy, O'Connor shows his more attractive side, and the Girl was pleased to see how charming it was. The men on that drive were probably not selected for their good clothes or their superior morals, but with an eye solely to their ability to get the logs along. They were officially classified as "white men, Irishmen, Province men, Bluenoses, Prince

Edward Islanders,[1] Canadian French, St. Francis, Micmac, Penobscot, and Passamaquoddy Indians;" but among all this mixed crew, in almost a week of familiar intercourse, not a man failed to be honest, orderly, and civil. Not a man was heard to swear, and the only impropriety of any sort was unwitting, and was promptly rebuked by several who could see, what the speaker did not, that it must be overheard. Boxes of camera plates, which would have been unbribable tell-tales to any meddling with the tent during long hours of absence, showed that not even an innocent curiosity ever went so far as to look at what was left in their keeping. In all ways they proved their good-will.

The Girl was charmed with other evidences of their kindliness. They were kind always to their great horses, which that year for the first time were used to draw the boats across the carry. The squirrels frisked about the wangan tents almost within arm's length of the cook.

[1] The last three were called P. I.'s, though, strictly speaking, a P. I. is a Prince Edward Islander.

The little birds were tame and numerous.
The wild hares seemed to know no fear.
One day the men found a fawn too young
to walk. They petted and talked to it,
brought it out to be seen, and then carefully left it where the mother would find
it again. A hermit thrush had built a nest
close beside the carry road, within the
camp-ground limits. She had selected that
spot before she knew that men and horses
and dynamite and millions of logs, thundering down over the falls, were to shake
the earth itself and break the sylvan stillness. She had not dreamed that twenty-six
great boats, drawn by heavy-footed horses,
clanking stout harness and straining at the
sledge whose runners clung to the bare
earth, were to be dragged past her little
house under the broken cherry-sprout
overarched with last year's bracken. Yet
she stoutly held her ground and stayed
upon her eggs, though only a rod away
passed the bustle of the drive. The nest
was pointed out to the men that they might
not accidentally crush it, and often they
would stand in the road and watch the little

bright-eyed mother, but not one of them ever startled her in order to see the eggs. When they were all gone and the carry was quiet again, she was still there under her little house, bright-eyed and confident.

The men were fond of flowers, too. Later in the season, when flowers are more abundant, the drivers will often be seen picking the harebells that grow upon the ledges, or a sprig of cardinal flower from the water's edge. If there is a pond lily to be had, it will be found twined into some driver's hat-band, or looped about his neck by its twisted stem. For some reason they had not noticed that clump of lady's-slippers at the Putting-in Place. There they lifted their heads in brave array, thick-set and green as to leaf, waxen and pure white as to petal. Perhaps the men avoided trampling on them, possibly they admired and left them on their stalks, but for some reason, neglect or conservation, no one disturbed them.

Up, down, and across that carry for almost a week flitted the Girl and her attendants, chatting, observing, photographing, fishing, idling in unalloyed delight through the longest and brightest of summer days, the guests of everybody. At any moment and at any point between Chesuncook Pond and Ambajemackomas, they were likely to appear, she with her camera, Wilbur with his rifle, and there was always some one right there ready to be of service. Big Oliver, the cook, had beans and biscuit to spare in any quantity,— and they were good. The men wanted to give her a chance to see how a jam is picked, and twenty of them picking off on the Little Arches insisted on standing still, that she might have a good chance to take their picture, while she as unweariedly waited for them to get into action. The men on the stations were always ready for a visit. There was an Indian boy, tribe and name unknown, who had plenty of time to spend a little hunting for a partridge's nest, which they never found, though they had some fun in hunting. There was a Province lad watching on the Little Arches when she came to wait there for the men to come down and pick a jam. He was on an island, to be reached only by walking a log across to the shore; but he must go ashore and hunt up the butt end of a log to make her a seat. Then because there was a cold wind drawing down the gorge, in spite of the warm June sunshine, he must go ashore several times to get wood to build a fire for her, by which they sat and chatted until she saw just what is that homesickness which takes a man engaged at dangerous work far off from home. Evenings, Joe Francis and Steve Stanislaus would come dragging wearily up the hill to eat a little supper at the tent, or to drink tea out of tin dippers as they lay about the fire and told stories, such stories that the echoes of their laughter may be heard yet hanging about the bluffs on Ripogenus. The morning after their arrival the Old Man came down, — he was not at all old, being the youngest of the three contractors of the drive that year; the name was a mere courtesy title. Out of his short time with his men he took almost half a day showing points of interest, explaining the technicalities of the work, telling old stories, acting as guide himself all the way across to the Big Eddy, three miles below, that nothing worth seeing should be missed.

Such a perfect excursion in the woods never was, and yet, although it did not trouble her, the Girl had noticed something strange. Wherever she appeared the men, if not too busy, seemed to be a little watchful; they were very careful of her; they treated her regardfully. She had the strictest orders never to go out of sight of her companions, and Wilbur always carried his heavy Winchester, which she knew was loaded. Is there danger in the house of one's friends? What possible harm could threaten a girl so protected by a universal good-will? She knew that she did not even need attendants on that carry, much less a rifle to defend her. There was nothing to shoot at that season. If there had been, they did not wish to shoot it. Moreover, it had been specially arranged not to bring a gun on the excursion. The girl was puzzled by this little cloud of apprehension which every one seemed to see except herself. It is the custom in the woods to obey orders and ask no questions: one who is keen arrives at conclusions in other ways, and " other ways " is precisely the woman's way.

The afternoon was hot, and it is a long trip down to Ambajemackomas and back to Ripogenus Lake. " What's the use, Wilbur, to carry that big forty-four seventy ? " said she. " The camera and plates are load enough ; it's six miles down there and not a step less back again, and we 've been down to the Big Eddy and back this morning. Better leave the rifle behind, had n't we ? "

There is no wile feminine so hard to fend against as a little friendly interest ; Wilbur was caught unprepared.

" There's nothing to shoot anyway at this season," said she, helping him out, as one does a trout with a landing-net.

" There's bears," said he rather desperately ; " you know June's just the season for bears to be running about."

She was entirely satisfied that it was not bears. She was not afraid of bears anyway ; yet she did not know what was the real reason for carrying the rifle, not knowing as much as everybody else did.

For Wilbur Webster, when he arrived at the carry, had brought down news; Mr. Murphy had verified it, and rumor therewith picked up the report and ran with it as only rumor can run, spreading everywhere that the Sunday before, this being Thursday, one Jack Russell had sworn openly in the 'Suncook House that if certain people came into the country where he was, he would shoot them on sight. Two days after that they appeared on the very spot where he uttered his threat, and it remained to be seen whether he would back down. The situation was not without interest at any time, but with a woman figuring in the title rôle, it was unique; certainly it appealed to the West Branch Drive. To have a scoundrel like Jack Russell threaten to shoot a lady who was their guest passed the limit. They were no longer critical spectators; the game was their own, and they played it with zeal.

Thereafter Wilbur became the centre of innumerable conferences, all semi-private.

"Do they know it?" was always the first question.

"I told *him* first off," was Wilbur's stereotyped answer. "We did n't want to spoil *her* good time, so he said to take my rifle, and we 'd see whether the woods was a free country."

"S'pose she suspects anything?"

"Should n't be so much surprised," replied Wilbur. "When she asked me why I lugged that big forty-four, I just floundered around in my mind for a minute; you can't lie to her quite as easy as you can to a sport, so I struck bears. 'Yes, there 's bears,' says she, kind of cool and twinkling. She knows as well as I do about how much bears are going to be bothering around this whole West Branch Drive."

"What 's he got agin *her*?" was another question.

Then Wilbur explained the origin of the grudge.

"Say, that so? Can she prove it on him?"

"I ruther guess she holds a full house on facts," modestly responded Wilbur, not

stating that he was the man who had supplied most of them, at some personal risk.

"Oh, it will stand law all right," said
Wilbur. They were waiting at the Putting-in Place among the men gathered to
meet the luncheon boy. That was why so
many men had leisure to stand and talk.
It is one of the sights to see the luncheon
boy come trotting along with his firkin of
salt beef and baking-powder biscuit in one
hand, and in the other an immense coffee-
pot, carried by a bail, while down his back
hang a double row of pint dippers strung
together by the handles, reminding one of
Jack Mann's saying that the worst load he
ever carried was five hundred pint dippers
without handles against a head wind. The
Girl could very easily amuse herself quest-
ing about after birds and flowers, while she
waited for a chance to get a photograph
of the luncheon boy.

"The law," went on Wilbur, the Girl
just now being out of range, "is just the
thing Jack Russell got too much of out
in the States; it's more for his health to
stay up here to 'Suncook where he ain't

reminded of jails. Your Old Man has got a warrant out agin him for assault, and the sheriff could have both hands full of papers if the complaints all came in to once. Jack Russell takes his settlements out of court, now you 'd better believe. Maybe what he said to me wa'n't nothing but guff, but maybe I ain't going to keep my eyes peeled for things moving the bushes t' other side the river ! "

" Oh, he ain't looking for trouble ; don't you worry, Wilbur," said one.

" No, I ain't worrying any; I 'm keeping my sights up for eighty yards *and* a few extry cartridges in my right-hand pocket."

A hunter's voice is always high-pitched, and a little excitement, which makes him forget his usual caution, will cause it to carry far. The Girl heard this last remark. She was some distance off one side, looking at some flowers.

" Oh, come here, Wilbur," she called ; "just look at this bunch of lady's-slippers ! Are n't they the prettiest ones you ever saw ? "

So Wilbur had to come and admire. It seemed to the Girl that there had been enough of a conversation which carried a man's voice up so high and made him forget his proper caution. What he was saying was very likely only "talk for P. I.'s" (which is a sort of buncombe), but that remark about the rifle-sights she bore in mind. She sat down and thought it all out at the next opportunity. She knew the butt end from the muzzle of a rifle, and knew that a hunter would not be likely to have the slide of his sights up for any such range; but what he had said seemed to have the ring of substantial truth about it, that he was prepared for a long shot. There are no long shots in the woods in June; one cannot see eighty yards then, unless there is open ground; here there was no open except along the river. One does n't go prepared to shoot bears across a raging river with inaccessible bluffs and no means of crossing. Besides, bears would never account for that stringent order never to get out of sight. She was beginning to perceive that here was some mystery.

What was it which Wilbur had told and Mr. Murphy had corroborated? That the Sunday before at the 'Suncook House, Jack Russell, " as mad as Mike," had spit forth his spite against certain people.

What was it about? Oh, about his killing rising twenty moose last summer for their hides; she had written something about it, and had sent him one of the papers with it in, so as to be fair.

" And if either of them ever puts foot into this country again I'm going to shoot 'em!" said Jack Russell.

" Well," spoke up Wilbur, who was among the crowd, " guess you won't have to wait long for your chance, Jack."

" How's that?" asked several.

" Oh, I hear," went on Wilbur as nonchalantly as if the letter announcing it were not in his pocket, " that they are coming up the Lake to-morrow, both of 'em."

" Where to?" asked Jack, wavering.

" Ri' down *here*, Jack." And the steel in Wilbur's voice must have rung clear.

" Who's goin' guide for 'em?" inquired Russell.

" *I* be, Jack ! " retorted Wilbur. Blades were out then. Wilbur was a proved man, and there was no mistaking what he meant.

This was too much for Jack Russell. He found it was just the right time to set some bear-traps up Harrington Lake way, which was miles out of the road of all tourists, far back in the woods. The whole of Chesuncook rippled with laughter at the performance, and then all subsided to a calm. What disturbed Wilbur was that Harrington lies on the further side of Ripogenus, quite a convenient distance for any one who wanted to stroll down for the day and, in some warm and mossy nook, to lie across an impassable chasm and take pot-shots at photographing tourists scrambling over the rocks on the other side.

Meantime the Girl knew next to nothing of what was going on. Here and there she caught some shred of conversation which, when raveled out, always gave the name of Jack Russell, and she wondered into what sort of stuff it had been woven, and especially what kind of goods could bear Jack Russell's name on every yard; it was considered no guarantee of quality at that time and place, for he came as near being a desperado as any one there in the woods. She did not think anything about Jack Russell, least of all would she have suspected that the drive was taking his threat seriously. It was enough that everybody was so kind, and that no one except once ever did anything which displeased her. That time she was angry — and then she was n't.

It was one noon coming back from the Big Eddy; it was hot, and to save time they were returning by the carry road instead of by the river-bank. At the Putting-in Place she looked for her clump of posies. They were missing. Not one was left.

A flame of anger burst forth at seeing them so despoiled. "It's a shame!" she cried; "I would n't touch one of them, they were so pretty, the prettiest moccasin-flowers that ever were, and now some one has gone and picked all that great bunch! Can't people ever learn to leave a pretty thing alone!"

Her anger had not cooled before there
came the dappled dawn of a new idea, and
she ceased to blame the spoilers until she
should be sure.

Men are fickle creatures, and those she
had seen here were about to be fed. If
they had picked the flowers to look at,
they would gaze at the waxy blooms a
moment, then roll them in their fingers
and, when the flowers hung limp and their
hands were full of meat and drink, they
would drop them where they stood. There
she would find the wilted, yellowing blossoms, with flabby, hanging pouch and drag-
gled, twisted pennons, telling the world-old
story of thoughtless ravage. She looked
all about. There were no flowers there.

Then she looked at the plants again,
more carefully. Their poor little denuded
stems stood up tall and stiff, full length;
every flower must have been nipped off
just beneath its little chin; it was not
done hastily, nor ruthlessly with the whole
hand, but deliberately, with thumb and
finger.

Then she blushed, neck and ears, redder than her hat. The doubtful dawn of her idea was full day now; she knew what had happened. For there came to her some chaffer on the way up from the Big Eddy. She had stepped in a muddy spot in the road, and they had told her, Wilbur and her father, that of the men who saw that track not one would ever efface it with his own; that sentiment still was dear to woodsmen. She had laughed and thereafter avoided the muddy places; one would not wish to put too great a strain upon sentiment. But now she remembered that when she had called to Wilbur, she had touched the flowers, lifting their heavy heads as she praised their beauty. That had sealed their doom. In eleven different pockets, pressed in the folds of a home letter or crumpled in the corner of a greasy pocketbook, the eleven little lady's-slippers were carried as keepsakes.

It is many years since that occurred, and yet she can never help feeling guilty for compassing the destruction of those pretty flowers; though glad that she can give to them a more enduring life.

That was not all, though she did not know it till long afterwards, when the clerk of the drive told the story. Wilbur's rifle was really not of the slightest consequence; it might just as well have been left in camp. For the West Branch Drive had taken upon itself to settle everything in its own thoroughgoing way. It decided — that is, enough of it decided, and there was no call for contrary-minded — that it objected to having Jack Russell interfering with its company. Then they discussed the matter of ways and means.

"Send him word," said one, and who so apt to be the man as the very one who had grumbled loudest about having women on the drive, "send him word to leave our company alone. If he don't, tell him we've got men enough and we've got rope enough" —

The message was somewhat pointed. It is quite a distance from Ripogenus up to Harrington, all woods, and P. L. D. runs no post-office department; but it was delivered with dispatch. When Jack Russell ran into us on the upper end of

Chesuncook Carry, a sort of head-on collision, before the Smiths of Chesuncook as outside witnesses, and it was fight, run, or be friends, he was entirely civil. Although too much must not be inferred from such a statement, we parted quite as cordial as when we met. However, Chesuncook shook with inextinguishable laughter; its merriment was both loud and long-continued, and it became so disturbing to Jack Russell's ears that by the time the leaves were falling, he turned his canoe prow northward, and was last seen going down the Allegash in search of a climate more congenial to his health.

VII

WORKING NIGHTS

WORKING NIGHTS

It was almost September, time for the logs to have been down in Argyle and Nebraska[1] and sorted, and here was North Twin Thoroughfare with two big booms choked in it. The little steamer that runs to the head of the lake was forced to lie by and wait for them, and aboard of her two old river-drivers, leaning against the pilot-house, were pouring contempt on all they saw. It was not conversation, but a series of snorts and snarls of disapproval, which, by study, could be disentangled into condemnation of — first, any company that could be so behindhand with their logs (for no such late drive as that of 1901 was ever heard of) ; second, any crew of men who would allow two booms to choke each other in a narrow thoroughfare ; and third, all men so imbecile as not to see the way to unsnarl the tangle.

[1] At Argyle, Nebraska, and Pea Cove booms, the logs are sorted by the log-marks of the owners.

The men upon the logs ran around aimlessly, like bewildered ants; they got a piece of spare boom, much too short, and with it lengthened one of the main booms; when it failed to relieve the congestion in the narrows, they did not know what to do; they tugged and pried and poked and hauled, they went sloshing and spattering and bouncing around on the logs, and nothing came of their labors. For four hours the little steamer lay there, and still the problem of those two booms was as great as in the beginning.

The veterans on the steamboat were entirely free in giving their opinions about the whole performance to every one but the men at work. To them they offered no suggestions. A calm aloofness characterized their demeanor.

" Any ten-year-old child could tell 'em what they 'd ought to do," said one of the old men to the other ; " all they 've got to do is just to cut both booms an' jine the ends of 'em, and they 'd slip those logs through them narrers like a cat goin' through a hole. Makes a heap of differ-

ence if there 's *two* cats both bent on gittin'
through at the same time ! "

"Course ! " agreed the other; " any fool
could tell 'em that, only half tryin' ; but
what do you expect of 'em this year, when
there ain't a single man on the drive that
knows the river ? "

I took the phrase home with me — not
a single man on the West Branch Drive
who " knew the river "! It was sheer impossibility, for there were always twenty
men at least, any one of whom could have
carried the whole drive down from Chesuncook to the boom. It had always been
the glory of the West Branch Drive that
it had so many men who had driven the
river for a score, for thirty, some for almost forty years. The men love that river
as they love no other ; it is the most difficult, the most dangerous, the most honorable post to be found, and the pride and
boast of the West Branch Drive has always
been, not its supple young foam-walkers,
who could traverse the froth of those white
rapids without wetting a shoe-tap, but its

battle-scarred boatmen, who "knew the river." For one who survived, many, it is true, had died young, but these older ones had all been lions in their day.

"Billy," said I, when I got home, speaking confidentially to one who had served his three and thirty years on the West Branch Drive, "where were you this spring — West Branch as usual ? "

"Oh, no," said he slowly, "I did n't drive this spring; I 'm gettin' most too old for that." He began river-driving at the ripe age of thirteen, though it was some years before he qualified as a West Brancher; and he probably would know how to handle a boat even yet.

"Where was Joe ? where was Steve? where was Joe Solomon? where was Prouty ? where was this one, that one, the other ? "

These were a dozen names that spelled West Branch in large letters. He shook his head at every name. — Where were they all ? Oh, at home ; all getting old like himself, or at some easier trade than river-driving, or off on East Branch working for

Con Murphy, who was a lumberman from the peavey up.

My sky had fallen. Never had I heard of anything more astonishing. Then light broke through a rift, but it was the light of a gray day. Times had changed. It was P. L. D. no longer; no longer the old " Company " for which our men had slaved so willingly; no longer Ross, Murphy, and Smart contracting for the drive; no longer any of the old neighborly names that we had always known ; no longer men above who had been the messmates and bunk-mates of those below ; no longer men below who obeyed orders only when they did not see a better way, who worked with all the strength there was in them, and on day wages were partners in interest and responsibility in as fine a piece of co-operative labor as any man can instance. The loudest grumbling I ever heard from river-drivers was not about their food, or their wages, or their long hours, but about being ordered to leave certain small parcels of logs which it would cost unduly to save ; they wanted to " leave the river all neat and clean;" they were anxious to do their work well.

The times had changed indeed. That year the great stranger company had taken the drive to show us how much better Millions of Money can manage those things. There was a railroad to its own doors; there were steamboats at its service on all the lakes; it had a telephone the length of the river; it had unlimited capital,— and all these our own leaders lacked, fighting the wilderness bare-handed. Besides, the Great Company very nearly owned the state: it owned the water-power; it owned the forest land; it guided legislation; it had made enormous improvements and was contemplating others which will end God knows where, if they do not improve us all out of existence. It was supreme, the incarnation of the Money Power, the eidolon of the Juggernaut Capital which is pictured as ready to crush all who will not bow down — and some who do. Never before had we seen anything which quite so boldly flaunted the legend, Money is Power. It could do what it pleased. It could buy what it pleased. It could buy everything.

Everything but men!

So not a single man of the old West Branch guard had bowed down to it, not a single man who knew the river had bent to its magnificence, but every man of them had shouldered his cant-dog and marched off to work for one who was "a lumber-man from the peavey up." It was superb. It was epically large.

The Millions of Money had it all their own way that year. The Great Company showed us many things about log-driving, chiefly by way of bad example. It has just had an opportunity given it in the courts to make partial reparation for its sins of ignorance. However these other damages fall out, that to its own reputation is quite beyond repair. It has been demonstrated that Money cannot drive logs, nor buy the men who can do it. The splendor of the Dollar, in public imagination at least, has suffered an eclipse.

But still the cost! Comrades of the peavey, that was your swan-song. Nevermore will you gather in the springtime, as you used to do, to fight the furious river for the logs committed to your care, raging like wild Achilles over his fallen friend; nevermore will you work eighteen hours a day and call it fun; nevermore toil for ninety days or a hundred without a break; nevermore (and here's the test) will you be called on to work nights. And I, never again shall I behold men looking like those I used to see when they came off the drive — white and Indian crisped almost to a blackness by the sun, baked with the heat, bitten by black flies, haggard, gaunt, sore-footed, so that, once their driving-boots were off, their parboiled feet could endure none but the softest kid or congress cloth, and even those I have seen them remove whenever they could; and above all sleepy, falling asleep while they talked to you, gaping from unutterable weariness, dropping into a dead slumber if left alone for a moment, and waking with a jump when anything stirred. In those days they worked both day and night.

Lewey Ketchum was talking with me about it. "They don't know how to work now, and they never will work again the way they used to. In those days we had breakfast and everything packed into the boats before it was daylight. You could hear them clinking things about in the boats before you could see the boats, if the morning was n't clear, and we were out on the logs before daybreak." One hardly needs to be reminded that in these northern latitudes dawn comes early in June.

"And then we used to work nights." That other, mark you, was just the day's work, even though it began not much after midnight. "We could do more work nights. Logs run faster then, can't tell why, but they do; so we used to sluice nights, and booming down the lakes was mostly done at night, — that is, we got along faster nights. If we had stopped to do it all by day, we would never have finished it, with the winds springing up. You see, we did n't have any steamers in those days, and the logs all had to be towed by hand. Now they 've got steamers on all the lakes, and the men think they can't do anything without them. They'll wait half a day to save an hour's paddling. But in the old times — well, you know it was hard and dangerous, but we did it because we liked it. It's a whole lot of *fun* to go into a bad place where you just know you can come out all right if something don't happen. You get to liking it. You get to wanting it when the year comes round. We always went on the drive just because we liked to be there, such a lot of men on the logs and all trying to get them along and beat each other, and all having a good time at it. It wasn't the pay " — (and no one ever supposed it was the pay, West Branchers, good though it was in those days) — " we didn't work just our money's worth. There was all those logs to be taken care of, and it kind of seemed as if a man *ought* to do the best he could. Everybody in those days did the best he could."

It is the testimony of an English Indian, Tobique bred; and I would that I might show you how, in placing the stress upon a question of duty where our own French-

descended Indians would have laid it upon
necessity, — a relic of the days of *il faut*
and *il doit*, what they " had got to do," not
what they " ought to do,"— I catch the
glow in Lewey's quarterings of the red
coat of Her Majesty's colonel, and hear the
echo, a hundred years and half the world
removed, of the cheers that answered Nel-
son's signal at Trafalgar. So fine a thing
as this that Lewey said must be unconscious. It shows clearly enough what their
work has done for these men's ideals. Hire
an old riverman to work for you, and there
will be little cause for complaint.

Two hundred and fifty [1] men, all doing
the best they could ! That was high en-
deavor, and it made manly worth. I know
that in their own words the West Branch
Drive "wa'n't no holy Sunday-school," and
with them the fireside moralities were often
lacking ; but over against their most shock-
ing breaches of morals balance the magni-
ficent *morale* of more than two hundred
men (not to mention the many hundreds

[1] The West Branch Drive numbered from 150 to 200
men at the start, and 250 or 300 men later when the logs
cut lower down had been received.

being educated on all the other drives) who were living sternly up to this high ideal of duty. When they died, they died doing their duty; when they lived, they carried back to field and forge and camp and trade the habit of doing the best they could; and the leaven of their example permeated the whole class till they tolerated no shirking, no "sogering," no unfaithfulness to a trust. The Penobscot man is a willing worker, capable in emergencies, true to his trust, knowing well the difference between "ought" and "ought not." And the drive was the college where he learned all this.

How much does a man working at day wages think he *ought* to do to earn his hire?

Here is the story Lewey Ketchum told me : it was rather a funny story, he said, — at least he told it for such, omitting much which I am bound to supply, and not suggesting that there was anything meritorious in what he did, because of course "a man ought to do the best he can." So many ellipses of information and explanation have to be filled in by me that I cannot reproduce his soft, cadenced English, wholly unlike our knotty Yankee idiom.

He was on Chesuncook — Gazungook, as he softened it, Indian fashion — in charge of a boom. It was the last boom of the rear, and he must not keep the crews waiting. There was no steamer there then, — there was none till 1891, — and all booms had to be towed by hand. Now Chesuncook is a lake eighteen miles long, and a boom comprised from two to five millions of feet of logs. To tow by hand such a heavy, unwieldy float of logs, many acres in extent, for so great a distance was always a work of magnitude. If the wind was contrary, it became by so much the harder; great loss of time might result from having to anchor under the shore; or of labor, from being carried back even to the starting-point; or of money, from logs rolling out from under the boom, or the boom itself parting and all its contents being spread abroad, a great portion of them never to be recovered. Delays were costly, the risks great, the labor terribly severe. Three days and nights it took, under favorable conditions, to warp a boom down Chesuncook, and it was heaving anchor all the way. Ask any sailor about work at the capstan bars, and then ask him what he would think of taking three days and nights of it without change of watches; probably he would tell you that it cannot be done. And yet it always was done in warping booms across our lakes, and one crew of men had to do it. Their meals were brought to them from the shore, and what little sleep they got they took upon the head-works; but there was very little sleep for any one unless they had to anchor under the lee of the land.

To make all clear, the great boom, made of logs linked end to end, having been stretched about all the loose logs it can safely hold, is made fast by a short warp to the head-works. This is a raft of triply cross-piled logs, one log long by about fourteen wide, all hewed to fit and stoutly treenailed together. Up to a recent date iron was too scarce in these remote outposts of the woods for any common use, and wood had to take its place; even at Chesuncook the booms were always double thorough-shotted with stout wooden pins instead of being linked with chains.

Upon the head-works raft was set the capstan, a great spool made of a single log, revolving about a central shaft, and pierced around the top for eight capstan bars. There were no pawls at the bottom, as on ship capstans, to prevent its surging back, but a number of small sticks slanting upward toward the barrel kept the warp from fouling under the spool. An anchor, seldom weighing over three hundred pounds, and about a thousand feet of inch and a half rigging are used in a warping boom. To judge of the weight of the warp, it is enough to say that, laid in coils with slack between, it takes twelve men, — the drivers at Ripogenus told me it would take fifteen men, — each carrying a coil upon his shoulder, to lug such a warp across a carry. These long warps are left behind, but I saw them carrying the shorter but heavier hawsers for sweeping the eddies, and as the undulating line crawled slowly up the hill, it looked like the folds of a great serpent. The anchor, the long booming-warp, the stout snubbing-hawsers, and a boat are the chief equipment of a booming crew. The anchor is boated out ahead and dropped; then all hands man the capstan bars, two men to a bar, and begin to spool up the warp. When the anchor is under-foot, the boom is left to drift with the headway already gained; twelve of the men boat out the anchor while the other four feed off the warp from the spool. Then the boat comes back, the men tumble out upon the head-works, and throw themselves upon the capstan bars, to begin their tramping around and around and around, as they wind up the straining warp. Thus, inch by inch, the boom is drawn across the lake, two or three miles in a day of twelve hours being all that a full crew at the bars can accomplish.

Lewey Ketchum's crew took their logs at Umbazooksus, the very head of the lake. It was about dusk when they tied their boat to the stern snubbing-post of the head-works and wound the first turns of the warp upon the windlass. They worked well, boating out, warping up, heaving anchor, inch by inch, foot by foot, by the main strength of their arms hauling along that great unwieldy float of logs. They made a path around the capstan where their spiked shoes tore out the splinters, — all within bright and new, all without new and bright, and that circle fouled with the wear of many spike-shod feet. That was the first night. Then the hawser began to bite into the barrel of the capstan, and left ridges where the heavy rope had jammed the fibres of the wood. That was the first day. Then the hawser began to show the fray of running over the front of the raft, and little pick-ends of hemp stood out from it. That was the second night. Then the men began to show it, men being tougher than wood and hemp, and able to stand more strain. They began to fall asleep at their work ; they began to drink strong tea to keep themselves awake, and, in spite of that, they nodded as they paced round and round and round the capstan, and fell fast asleep, still working, never forgetting to step a little higher as the warp rose with each revolution, but moving more slowly because they were asleep. That was the second day. Yet their work was but two thirds completed. The third night was coming.

Not that Lewey Ketchum let his men work thus continuously without rest or change. He knew too well how to get work done to make that mistake. There came sometimes a little breeze favoring them, and then Lewey had some spreads laid down and made his men turn in. They lay down like a basket of kittens, curled up all sorts of ways, but kept from rolling off by the bulwark around the head-works. Glad enough were they for the rest and sleep, yet before they took it they made a sail out of another of the great woods spreads, ample enough to cover twenty men, stretching it upon light poles put up before the capstan. Sometimes the breeze would last an hour or two, and the raft would sail as far as if they had been

manning the capstan bars all the time.
Then the breeze would die away, or it
would draw down Cuxabexis, or it would
be openly unfavorable, and then once more
it was " Turn out, boys ! " and the anchor
was laid out ahead and the capstan groaned
again. But the men had been refreshed,
and came to their task as good as new.

But not so Lewey. He never shut his
eyes. While the others slept, he watched.
They might get refreshment; he must go
to the end of his task without it. The
men offered to take his place and give him
a chance to sleep. He knew their good-
will, and also how, having had a little sleep,
they would fall back into it all the more
readily. No man could take his responsibility, and he would let no man take his
place. That was the last boom of the rear ;
if that were carried back, the whole drive
must wait for it, and he would risk nothing.
So there he sat watching while the rest
slumbered.

It may have been that they had a lantern on the corner of the raft to guide the
boat in boating out ; it may have been, as

in old times, that upon a graveled space they had built a little fire, and that there as formerly they kept a kettle of tea, which boiled day after day, the grounds never emptied, but a new handful and a fresh supply of lake water added whenever the supply ran low. By the third night this would have tanned sole leather: it was very nearly strong enough to keep a man awake. One can see that Lewey must have gone to it often, not for the tea, nor that it should keep him awake, but just to make an errand. It is so still and quiet broad off in a lake at night that if one sits, making no movement, although not asleep at all, he falls into a moon-gaze and, being quite conscious, is yet unable to move; he sits rigid, and his soul wanders off upon the waters and cannot get back again into his body. That is just as bad as being asleep.

There was little enough to see. The stars were out in northern clearness, and, as the night lagged on, he saw the Virgin pace across the sky, following the sickle of Leo and the Twins, and down the lake

he saw the Scorpion rise, with upraised
sting and red Antares in his head. But
the stars are a silent folk, indifferent company to one who does not know them
well. Of sounds which he did know there
were few enough. There was the wash of
the ripple along the logs, the creak of the
thorough-shots, groaning occasionally, the
slacking of the big quilt if it spilled a little
of the breeze. A horned owl hooted twice
from the shore; a fish jumped once; a
night-flying wild duck steamed past at full
speed, whippering his wings just over the
water, and once, off the mouth of Caribou,
a loon lifted his voice in a long and deso-
late cry. Yet the sounds came so seldom.
All that made it seem that he was not
floating midway between the stars burning
above him in the sky and those twinkling
below him in the glassy lake was the fire
on the corner of the raft and the sterto-
rous breathing of fifteen tired men asleep
behind him. The loon called again. He
wondered if it betokened a change of wind.
He dipped his finger in the lake and held
it up to catch the breeze. The wind had

died away. "Turn out, boys!" came the word. Already the morning star was paling all her sisters; it was almost time for breakfast on the drive, and the crew was ready to go to work with new spirit.

Perhaps Lewey could rest now, for they were getting well along toward the piers. But Lewey could not rest. It was his boom to see safe in, and until he had given up the charge of it, accidents might happen. The crew were waiting for that last boom of logs, and he must not fail them. Lewey must work, and work as hard as any of his men, for the boss of a driving crew never wears kid gloves; all his authority comes to him from going where no one else dares go, from beginning first and quitting last, from doing the most work in the best manner.

So Lewey braced to the handspikes and began to heave on the anchor. He did not even doze while he walked round and round the capstan. He was too far gone for that. There was a little fever no doubt, and some twitching of the nerves, but he was very strong, and he moved on springs;

people feel that way when they have gone without sleep long enough. He did not always answer quickly to the men; he did not hear them, — the veins in his temples sang too loud for clear hearing; but there was no man who could do more work. When he got his boom down where it was to be turned out for sluicing, he had been three full days and nights without sleep, and most of the time working at the hardest sort of labor.

It was getting along toward supper-time when they went up to the carry. Lewey saw that his men had something to eat, and told them to turn in. It did not matter if it was not dark; they could sleep anywhere now, and had earned an extra allowance. They turned in, and in two minutes were as sound asleep as rabbits.

Now comes what Lewey called the funny part of his story. A good deal of the above he did not tell me. He spoke as to a comrade who could supply all the details, which accordingly I have supplied, because I know what must have been true. He himself sped straight to the point that after three days and nights he could not sleep. It was all so noisy on the carry. Men came and went, and they shook the ground so. He did not hear them much, but he felt the ground shake. And the little birds made such a cheeping and bother about going to bed; their small voices were pitched high, so that he could not help hearing. As the dusk fell and the evening star grew golden, the frogs peeped and piped, and an old bull-paddock[1] off somewhere bellowed like a moose in October. After that the men were restless, lying in a long line under their shelter tent. It sounded like the bellows and the forges of an anchor factory to hear them. His wrists throbbed and he could hear his heart and the pulse in his temples, and he could not close his eyes because he could see so many things. It was like looking under the ocean through a water-glass, he could see so many things which no one else could see. Not a wink of sleep did he get, and that the fourth night.

His men turned out fresh and bright.

[1] A local and ancient name for the bullfrog.

"Had a good sleep ; makes a man feel fit," said they, stretching their arms.

Lewey felt weak in his arms, and he had no appetite for beans. His men looked solicitous, — offered rude kindnesses, bade him loaf for the day and see if idleness could not unstring his nerves. After some hours of hanging about the wangan and the carry-end, it seemed to him that, if he could get off somewhere where it was quiet, he might perhaps go to sleep. Indian-fashion, he said nothing about his intentions, but took a little spread, his own private property, for he never liked to use the bedding common to the crew, and along in the morning he started off into the woods. He went perhaps a quarter of a mile, till he could hear neither the logs, the lake, nor the men, and found a smooth, dry spot among the trees. The birds did not cheep so loudly as they had done earlier in the morning, and it was quiet and calm there. Lewey wrapped himself up head and ears, — any one who has ever camped with him knows how like a great gray chrysalis he can make himself appear, a human *Cecropia*, covered with dew, dead twigs, and dry leaves, which, in a night of sleeping out, adhered to his blanket cocoon; one would never think there was a man inside, but expect it to hatch a mammoth butterfly. Even after he got all rolled up, he kept on seeing things as before; but in a quarter of an hour he ceased to realize that he was living in a glass case a mile above the earth, a kind oblivion stole over him, and he slept.

That was the last Lewey knew. There is no means of measuring time in sleep, and when we wake, even from the sleep of death, it will always be the next morning. When he waked it was because an unexplained hunger gnawed him. He felt quite himself, not very strong perhaps, but fresh and bright and able to hear things properly. The sun was getting near meridian; he calculated that he had had four hours' sleep. He had not eaten any breakfast, he remembered, and that quite accounted for his friendly feeling toward the cook. So he took his spread upon his shoulder and went back to the carry.

But there he was Rip Van Winkle: there was not a man there; there was not a log there; there was not a boat; there was no one at the dam; every single thing was gone; the ashes of the fire were cold, the blackened embers lay dispersed, the cross-bills were pecking around the empty pork barrels for the salt, and the red squirrels stretched their necks from behind old camp-wood, wondering if they dared come near enough to snatch a coveted morsel of stale bread. Lewey was dumfounded. He had left a large crew here when he went to sleep, and now the rear had cleaned up everything; they had hidden the anchors and carried off the warp and gotten the last barrel of wangan out of the way, and no one had been across the carry that day. He could not tell how long he had been asleep, — a day, two days, a week, — nor whether he should come up with the crew at all before the logs were all in boom.

He took his spread by the centre, and holding it with the corners dragging down his back, he set off down the carry. It is half a mile across; when he got to the lower

end he could see, almost down to the out-
let of Ripogenus Lake, the first signs of
human life, two head-works, one on either
side, warping down the rear. It is quite a
cry across that lake, and as there was no
boat awaiting his convenience, Lewey took
the path along the right-hand shore. It
was almost noon, and he was faint and
dizzy, but there was nothing else to do. It
was not till he was well down toward the
carry that any one discovered him. Then a
shout went up.

"There's Lewey!"

"See there! that's Lewey now!"

"Say, Lewey's found *himself* all right."

"Hello, Lewey! been padouksi?" —
which is to say, sleepy.

"Well, sleepy-head, tell us, is it to-day
or to-morrow?"

They made him the butt of all sorts of
jokes, but seemed uncommonly glad to
see him. Lewey did not say it, of course,
but he was always a prime favorite on the
drive, and it seems that they had become
alarmed on his account.

They had been worried when he did not

appear after a reasonable time ; they had
become most anxious when he delayed un-
reasonably, for there in the dew and the
dead leaves and the silvery spiders' webs,
the bright sunshine and the green leaves
blotched with yellow light, Lewey Ketchum
had slept a whole day and a night and a
half of a day again. The drivers had done
some nine hours' work on their second
day before he showed himself. Meanwhile
some accident was feared, and they had
hunted for him everywhere. Dazed with
loss of sleep, he might have tumbled into
the lake, and they searched the water round
the dam. Or he might have wandered off
into the woods, and half the crew had been
out whooping and hallooing to call him in.
Then they thought that, crazed with sleep-
lessness, he might be in such condition
that he could not understand their uproar
even if he heard it, and might wander hope-
lessly and perish in the wilderness. So they
had sent men all the way through to the
Grant Farm to spread the news of a man
lost.

And all that time Lewey was quietly

sleeping within rifle-shot of the camp.
Being an Indian and a hunter, he had
known how to hide himself, and being en-
veloped head and ears in his spread, the
trump of Gabriel would not have roused
him, even if all the lesser angels had joined
in the fanfare.

"It was," so Lewey told me, laughing,
"very funny." But about a man's working three days and nights without sleep,
because he was a day laborer on other men's
property and thought it was his duty to
do the best he could, Lewey had nothing
to say : that was all part of the day's work.
It was customary in those days for a man
to do the best he could.

The Great Company can train all that
out of our men : we are quick to learn.
We heard the evidence in the big log case
which for four days was a school of the
woods to the people of Bangor, and it was
plain enough that there was a difference.

The Great Company was, in polite legal
terms, requested to answer to a question
of tort for the loss of logs committed to

its care in the year 1901, the same being
due to willful neglect or to gross incompe-
tence. A lawyer could put it much less
candidly, but that was the popular impres-
sion from the evidence. Actions for tort
for log-cases were such a novelty that this
proved a sensational attraction; nearly
everybody was there to hear and to form
an opinion. The fourth day of the trial,
the interest growing rather than abating,
they had upon the stand a witness who was
a lumberman "from the peavey up." He
was an expert; almost forty years he had
put in on the river as master and man.
When he used to go on the drive, he testified, the crews did their best work sluicing
at night, but "nowadays they don't seem
to work much nights." The spectators
laughed, — so many of them had worked
on the logs themselves; they felt so strongly
for the old times and burned so hot against
the new. The counsel for the defense fluttered at the phrase and objected, — he, too,
understood, — and the offensive clause was
stricken out.

They do not work much at night now,

it is true. Whose fault? There is no need of it, — and that is well. But in the old time, when they did it because a man *ought* to do the best he can, the example of faithfulness to a trust was set them by their leaders, and they made a fair copy of it. They were quick to imitate, — and they had never heard about actions of tort, — and they were silly enough never to weigh their labor over against their duty.

It was the requiem of the West Branch Drive that Con Murphy sang when he said that " nowadays they don't seem to work much nights." Great Corporations get only what they pay for, or a little less ; what men slave for, die for, work nights for, is an Ideal, an Example, and a Man.

VIII

THE NAUGHTY PRIDE OF
BLACK SEBAT AND OTHERS

THE NAUGHTY PRIDE OF
BLACK SEBAT AND OTHERS

I was more than a little angry with the
man. He lived in such a nice and finick-
ing world, where every virtue was scrubbed
and dusted to the last degree and then
set on a shelf marked "Please do not handle," — real Dresden shepherdesses of
virtues, of no use to any one. Of the rough
and tumble of qualities, good and bad, in a
mucky world, and the way in which some
of the best of them become besmeared with
vices and yet all the while are big, living,
breathing, life-engendering virtues, he had
no comprehension. A diamond in the
rough was no diamond at all to him.

I told him frankly that he lacked eyes.
He could not see it so, — the blind never
can; yet here he was, in his blindness,
complaining of our lacking sentiment.

"You know nothing whatever about it,"
I returned rather hotly.

His looks said, "You are very rude, but I am too much a gentleman to say so."

(One who was a little less a gentleman and a little more a *man* would have come up gladly to that challenge, I thought; either he did know or else he did not — why evade the point?)

"What has brought our logs in for the last fifty years has been very nearly one third pure sentiment," said I, challenging again.

"That's nonsense," he objected.

"Their ideals" — said I.

"The-ir i-*de*-als," he drawled, and the repetition was cynicism rouged and powdered; "and what, pray, leads you to suppose that they have any i-*de*-als?"

I had a choice of evils — to retire in anger, nominally defeated, or to argue down one who could never see the point.

"I can prove it," I asserted.

"And *I doubt* it," he returned suavely. "I-*de*-als! My eye and Betty Martin! What do such rough fellows know about ideals? They know nothing but rum and fighting and sickening displays of silly bravado! Have n't they any faults, these rivermen of yours?"

I saw my opening. "Ye-es," said I, remembering Sam Weller and looking metaphorically at the skylight; "there is no doubt but they are proud."

"Which undoubtedly, like all the rest, is pardonable?" He was ironical.

"Which may be left to others to judge whether it is pardonable or not; there is no question of its being black pride. While you are about it, you may as well prepare to modify your opinionated doubts" — that was rather good, "opinionated doubts," almost an epigram — "concerning sentiment in log-driving and the ideals of log-drivers. It will be no harder to admit one of my points than all."

"No, no harder," said he, blandly irritating. "Go on with your story."

By the way that he slipped down into his chair and made himself comfortable with a palmleaf fan before his eyes, I wondered whether he was not preparing to be bored. But then, how could any one help enjoying Black Sebat? To think of him is to have a little warmer feeling toward the world, and to forgive some of its shortcomings.

Can any one who is old enough to remember so far back ever forget that hot, dry summer of the Centennial year? A hot July, and a hot and rainless August, and a September hotter than either. It was beautiful, but one drooped under the merciless pelting of the sun. Even the last of September, train-loads of sight-seers, returning from the great exposition, full of pride, patriotism, and enthusiasm, anxious to talk to fellow-travelers of the wonders they had seen, gasped mute in the cars, and with every door and window open, coatless and collarless, regardless of all proprieties, hung limp upon the arms of their own car-seat, or the back of the one in front.

Such a train-load was crossing the Connecticut River at Springfield; it was not a river, merely a gravel-bed with a few pools of water here and there.

"Ma! ma!" shrilled a boy, no more pervious to the heat than a cicada, "what's the matter with that river?"

"The only trouble with that river," said a passenger, willing to relieve the tired mother, "is that the bottom is too near the top; otherwise that is a very good river."

That was the year, and the river was in that condition, when John Ross made his great Connecticut River Drive. Only two days before that train-load of tourists crossed, he had gotten it out safe, past all the hazards of drought and heat. The men talk about that drive yet. "And they made a song about that drive," says your guide, squatting before the frying-pan with his uplifted fork raised like a tuning-fork; "I disremembers the whole of it, but there was something in it about

> 'Old Burke he gave a whoop,
> Harrigan gave a swagan,
> And Black Jack gave a soup.'

That's all I can think to tell you about that song now, but that drive of John Ross's it was a great drive, and that about the song is all so; you need n't not doubt a word of it, for Black Jack did make a soup just the same way that song says." He spears the bacon in the frying-pan and drives it around a little, as if he were handling big pine. "But that drive was a great drive all the same," says he.

Why John Ross and the West Branch Drive were off on the Connecticut River that year; how they got the logs through on a river of such length, with no storage of water, in the face of such a drought; how they beat out fearful friends and taunting foes and strangers who were betting high on its being an impossibility, and all for the honor of the Penobscot name, is a story too large to be pictured on this little page. They all toiled terribly from early spring till mid-September, the longest drive ever heard of up to that date; and had the men been forced to come home beaten, there is no telling what they would have done, but it would near have broken their hearts. If they had not had child's faith and man's faith in John Ross, and if he had not known just the stuff that was behind him and what they would do for him, — if, in short, there had not been a general at the head and a miniature army behind, they never could have taken that drive through. It was a great drive.

My father was with that train-load of people that hot day when the boy asked what was the matter with the river. He was the one who explained the difficulty. Such a day as that he thought he had never experienced in all his life, the most of it spent out of doors. It was the heat of a strange country, the drought of a foreign land, among people who, though charmingly kind, were not quite of kin ; it was all unlike the home country, and in two weeks — he took particular notice — he never heard a man swear.

He arrived in Boston, and in half an hour he was home again. A chill sea-wind was blowing, which made him reach for his overcoat. There was a tonic smell of salt in the air. On board the steamer, crowding about the bows, were thirty or more Penobscot river-drivers, the first to arrive or the last to get through celebrating, just off from Ross's Connecticut River Drive. He chronicled the fact that all he had lost in the way of swearing in those last two weeks was made up to him within fifteen minutes, with a considerable surplus to put out at interest. However, he was right at home, and he had need to be an octopus, or a polypus, or Briareus the hundred-handed, to take all the hands that were stretched out to him. So they got him in the centre of the circle, and those who knew him crowded round where they could clap him on the shoulder when a hand was lacking, while those who did not know him stood one side and very politely looked at the toes of their boots. Everybody talked at once.

"Hullo, *Man*ry!" That was an Indian, with a big slap on the shoulder.

"Say, glad to see you, Manly,"—crisp and clear, and that was a white man, with a handshake.

"My soul, but we ben berry much blessed for seen you," — from an Indian again, holding out both hands.

"Well, by jings! where did they rain *you* down from, Manly?" — the hearty greeting of a white man.

Then little Sebattis Solomon pushed up for his turn. "By jolly, but we just so glad seen our own brudder!" That was Black Sebat, who never had a brother that any one ever heard of.

There is no lack of heartiness in a river-driver if he is a friend of yours, and these were typical of their class, newly fledged from the slop-shop most likely, but still wearing their spike-soled boots, and not asking the officers of the steamer whether or no it was agreeable to the management. (All boat and train officials coming into Bangor had long since learned not to offer advice upon that subject unasked.) They were cheerful, if not actually inebriate, but orderly enough, and they were proud and very happy; there was no keeping to themselves their satisfaction at getting that drive in.

"She got it his dribe in all right John Loss; I tell you *we done him!*" announced little Sebat, grinning and shining all over his dark face. They called him Black Sebat and Old Black. He was a short, small man, as black as Sambo, hardly more than a feather-weight, but incredibly strong and wiry. He could tend sled all alone, the

only man, an old lumberman said, that he
ever saw who could do it, for that is two
men's work. And he was devoted to the
West Branch Drive and John Ross. That
was the first thing he wanted to talk about.
" Dem logs she ben all hung up, ain't for
us," he declared. There was more evidently on his mind; one who knew Sebat
could tell when he was preparing to make
known some feat of his.

" What did I hear about running Canaan Falls?" asked my father, making a
good guess at it.

" Ah, ya-as, dem Sappiel Orson an' Sebat Clossian she ben gone over Canaan
Falls," beamed Sebattis, trying to be non-
chalant.

" Dem Mitch Soc Francis she ben
drowndit herself," he went on earnestly,
drawing a step nearer to his theme.

" Whose boat was it that went over?"
asked my father, perceiving that but one
man more needed to be accounted for, and
that Sebattis had not mentioned the bowman; he could make a shrewd guess who
was bowman from the way Sebat acted.

Sebattis's face shone, beamed, was wreathed in smiles; he just stood and radiated good nature. "You heard it 'bout dat? Well, by jolly!"

But Sebattis had been too much the centre of attention. In some ways a crew of woodsmen reminds one of a pack of hounds, good-natured and peaceable fellows, each willing for the others to have some praise, but wanting his own share, too, and crowding up to get it. The individual feat of running Canaan Falls was suddenly side-tracked, and that other more general one of getting the Connecticut River logs into boom was brought to the fore.

"If that drive had n't 'a' got in, I — I — I donno!" said a tall white man with a pale yellow mustache bristling from a brick-red countenance, as he gazed out over the bay and thoughtfully bit off a large chew from his plug. "And my fare back all paid — but I — I donno!"

"Oh, I tell you, when we t'ought we was goin' ben beat we swear jus' lak hell, sac-er-r-ré-*damn!*" said a Frenchman, a stranger, who had interestedly worked himself into the inner circle. " But I tell you, dat John Ross he 's great old boy; she 's ben all hung up good, down b'low— b'low what you call it Hollowyoke; she 's all done for, high 'n' dry, an' then she jus' blas' it out channel and took hees whole dribe t'rough ! "

That was the fact. At the very time when, down in Hartford, the loiterers and gamblers were laying heavy bets that the drive was a dead failure, John Ross was blasting out a channel in the waterless river, and he took his logs through all right. The men were jubilant. It was their success. It was a Penobscot triumph. It meant to them all that a great victory means to an army, and though they stood in Boston, on foreign ground, were they not still the West Branch Drive, the greatest drive that ever was, the drive that could n't be beaten? Pride, pride, pride! they might try to look stupid, they might deceive one who did not know them, but no exultant college crew ever failed more signally to appear meek before the eyes of its friends.

It happened later, when my father had
gone inside for his overcoat and was up-
stairs in the main saloon, that carved and
gilded and Corinthian-columned saloon of
the old Cambridge, that one of the Indians
came strolling through to find him, not
quite steady in his mind nor on his feet, and
yet following as a dog follows a trail that
is familiar. There were ladies and there
were children about, and to the unaccustomed eye Joe looked a little wild ; he was,
moreover, — that is, he could hardly be
called half-seas over, for he was fully two
thirds of the way across the bay ; but when
he caught sight of my father, he grinned
with contentment and came up like a smil-
ing, wagging dog who loves his friends and
can't begin to tell them how much. Joe
wanted to talk. He wanted to talk confidentially. So when he was persuaded to sit
in one of the upholstered chairs, Joe put
an arm about my father's neck and began
in stage whispers which could be heard all
over the saloon. The ladies looked a trifle
perturbed at first, not being used to anything less decorous than a cigar-store In-

dian, but seeing that no harm came to the deacon, they soon settled their plumage and turned observers. Joe talked on, telling a long story, and hugging my father tighter and tighter. He was telling the story of the boat's crew that ran Canaan Falls. It was a reckless, unheard of, inexplicable folly. In time he gave a reason, good and sufficient, but his first reply was also memorable.

"What made them do it, Joe?"

And Joe, 'eyes shining, beaming wide, trumpeted in his sepulchral whisper, "Well, you see, Oldtown Injun she's damn praoud!"

Just so. There's no group of slouching rivermen idling about a corner, with their hats pulled down over their eyes, but among them, wherever you find a man good at his profession, you will find also, if all his faults were written on his forehead, as the proverb says, that he is "damn proud."

Joe said more. Just because he said it that afternoon in the saloon of the old Cambridge, steaming along toward home, and because it fell into the ear of one who

for eight and twenty years has remembered
it word for word, his comrades, whom every
one condemned for an act of drunken rash-
ness, shall be justified. A man must be in
some way beside himself to be a pure ideal-
ist, just enough the fool or madman to be
above the more immediate tug of self-in-
terest. Even though that release came to
these men by the way of a vice, their virtue
was none the less a virtue. In due place
I shall tell what Joe Orson said.

How came the West Branch Drive off
on the Connecticut River? Because John
Ross had contracted that year to take down
all the logs on the river, from headwaters
to Hartford. But if there were logs on the
West Branch to be run, why were not the
men who did that the West Branch Drive?
which is a sensible enough question. Nominally they were; every drive takes its name
from the river it is made on. Yet in a peculiar way, shared by no other river, the
West Branch Drive was an entity, the pro-
duct of the genius of John Ross. The other
drives were made up of good men, who

worked by the day; but the West Branch Drive was a little army, drilled and commanded by a military genius, and its virtues were preëminently the virtues of fighting men. For fifty years John Ross worked on the river, for about thirty he was one of the heads, when he was not sole head, of the West Branch Drive, and he trained his men to a degree of efficiency never known before. They came to believe that there was no place on the earth or under it that the West Branch Drive could not take logs out of, if John Ross gave the word.

Consequently, the Penobscot man fell into the sin of pride. He had no dealings with the Kennebecker; he scorned the Machias man; he made life a burden to the P. I. Deep down in all of us, like the ineradicable wildness of a cage-bred wild beast, lies this fierce, intractable pride of the River. That is why I have called this book "The Penobscot Man," because I know that wheresoever he may be, he is not going to forget his river. On my first train journey, as a little child, when we were riding up the Kennebec, I remember making friends with the lady across the aisle, and explaining to her that I lived on a river, too, "a great deal bigger and a great deal nicer.river than that river; mine was the Penobscot River"—and she, poor woman, was a Kennebecker! It is a very naughty pride, yet how strong it is in the men who are rivermen! The poor Kennebecker, years ago, when he used to come here to work, was the butt of all sorts of contumelious jokes. In the days when our men carried their gear in an old meal-sack, his enameled cloth or flowery carpet-bag was dubbed in ridicule a "Kennebecker;" and everything awkward was laid at the door of the stranger as a "Kennebec swing." In his wake the P. I. has suffered all sorts of reviling, and well for him when he is either an exceptionally able man or a very meek one.

"I'd like to know what there is about that name 'P. I.,'" said a Western college man to me. "We had a fellow from down your way, and we always called him 'P. I.'—'P. I. Murchison'"—or something else. "It didn't mean a thing to us, but when we found it vexed him, we kept it up; but what was there in that to get roiled about?"

"Why did n't you," I asked, "call him Irish, or a Dago, or some soothing term? Why needlessly enrage a Penobscot man by calling him a P. I.?"

Yet, once the men from away are broken in, there is no more of this rough-carding. If they are good enough men to belong to the West Branch Drive, the real meat and marrow of it, then all distinctions of race and place are forgotten. There never was a more democratic organization on earth: all our head lumbermen have been bossed first or last by Indian boatmen, and have started at the foot of the ladder without favors. All the good men are Penobscot men. The name stands for something. Let there be trouble on the other rivers, let the logs be given up by the local crews, they would send over for a hundred or two Penobscot men. Then all the old West Branchers would enlist, and march off and clear out that drive — and everything else they met on the road. Oh, the men have told me all about those old days !

Therefore when John Ross contracted for the Connecticut River Drive, he took over all his Maynard boats and a hundred and fifty of his old men. Plenty of other men could be had fit to step-and-fetch-it, plenty of boats good enough for some uses, but for the solid core of his drive he took men whom he had trained himself, Yankees, Frenchmen, Indians, Province men, but all Penobscot. They would follow John Ross anywhere; they would do for him what will never be believed when the traditions once have faded. He was that rare creature, the idol of his men. " The King of the River," I have heard him called by a college man who had worked on the logs in vacations and knew of what he spoke. Nor is his a purely local reputation. To-day, off in the Northwest among the great logs of Puget Sound, or down in the Southwest in some mining-camp or on some cattle ranch, you shall some day overhear a man who speaks of "joining drives," or who talks of a "plant"

as an "operation," or who promises "to
tend out" on court or a church social. If
you are blunt, you will say, "Hello,
Maine!" and get a blank denial; but if
you are subtle in your mind and know
your native tongue, even when meeting it
in unaccustomed places, when you recognize the Penobscot man, let fall casually
to your companion something about John
Ross and what old Jack Mann said to him,
even if you have to make it up out of
whole cloth.

"And where did *you* ever hear of John
Ross?" says he, hooking himself at your
first cast.

"Where did *you?*" you return, the back-
question being the proper Yankee retort.
"*I'm* Penobscot"—not "from the Penobscot," for that would brand you an
impostor, but just the barest phrase, "I'm
Penobscot."

"So'm I!" he says, which you knew
well enough before; "what was that you
were saying about John Ross?" He ends
by inviting you to his house, his mill, his
ranch, his assay office, and the next time

he sights you across a street, he comes over and begins just where he left off talking—about John Ross.

We never had but two men who took hold of the popular imagination in that way. The first was old General Veazie, who built one of the first railroads in New England. Forty years, perhaps, after he died, I heard a man get up in an orthodox prayer-meeting and say of some character (whether in the Bible or out of the Bible I shall not tell), that that man "felt so big that General Veazie's great-coat would n't make a vest for him." That was fame.

Concerning the second, perhaps to-day, if you are going along the streets of Oldtown, you may see some small boy mount a pile of lumber and clap his arms and crow, "Hi-i-yi! John Ross on a clapboard!" or "John Ross on a shingle!" or he may look saucily up into your face and exclaim, "Say I 'm John Ross, or I 'll kill you!" That, too, is fame! There is no longer any West Branch Drive; the Great Company has seen to that and swept away the old organization where friendly rivalry and fraternal discipline held the men together in a Round Table of noble and unceasing adventures. But it will take more than the Great Company to stop the mouths of the little boys of Oldtown. Fifty years from now,—just as to-day, under the name of Pope Night, the children of Portsmouth, New Hampshire, celebrate Guy Fawkes' Day, the children being the great conservers of old tradition,—fifty years from now, and very likely more, you will hear the little boys of Oldtown crying out, "Say I 'm John Ross, or I 'll kill you!" And that will be fame!

So much of exposition of how we came to have the sin of pride; by way of illustration we have Sebattis Solomon. Sebattis could well illustrate several other sins, though it will be by his virtues that he is remembered. In trying to make clear what Sebat was like, no illustration seems so apt as that of an old-fashioned home-made rubber ball, the centre of pure rubber, tough as gristle, wound hard with homespun yarn, a thread of white and a thread of black, but so commingled that without unwinding the whole no man might tell how much of it was black and how much was white, and so endowed with resilience that the harder it was hit the higher it bounced. You could no more keep Sebattis Solomon down than you could keep down one of those round-ended rubber dolls that bob up from all positions and balance anywhere.

What a quaint dignity he had, priding itself in all sorts of unexpected places! Once my father was remonstrating with him for being drunk. They were the best of friends, but Sebattis stiffened immediately. "Must n' you said dat, Manry!" he commanded. "Must n' you nebber said Sebattis Solomon she's drunk! 'Cause you see, she *can't be done!*"

Pride at times became a childlike vanity, as when he got his employer to write a letter which contained nothing but the news, four times repeated, that Sebattis Solomon was driving four white horses. "You got it dat wrote down? Well, den you told him 'Sebattis Solomon she's

dribe it four white horses.'" Immediately
came the question again, "You got it dat
wrote down? Well, we want for tell it
how Sebattis Solomon she's dribin' four
white horses."

Yet for some notable feat of skill or
endurance he would refuse both thanks
and pay. Once when the drive was at
Northeast Carry and some article of necessity was desired at once which could not
be procured nearer than Greenville, Sebat
took a heavy canoe upon his head and ran
across the carry two miles and twenty
rods, to Moosehead Lake. There he
threw the canoe into the water and started
out forthwith, late in the afternoon, to
paddle against a heavy wind to Greenville, forty miles away. He arrived in the
middle of the night, routed out whoever
could get him what he came for, and set off
at once to paddle back his forty miles,
after which he again lugged his canoe
across the carry, arriving early in the day.
He was a small man, not weighing over a
hundred and twenty, and he had lugged
four miles and more, and paddled eighty,

without rest and almost without food. What was to pay? "Oh, she's 'bout day's work; s'pos'n' we call it t'ree dollar." Hervé Riel's half-holiday and leave to go and see his wife was princely compensation to what Sebattis asked.

Sebattis knew well the struggle of two natures. His notions of right and wrong were firmly implanted, and in his own way he tried to live up to them. Once he came bringing as a gift a crooked knife which he had made, the blade ground down from an old file, the handle most elaborately carved. "You see, she's 'gainst our principles," — (no one loves a long word better than an Indian,) — "'gainst our principles hunt on Sunday; took us t'ree Sunday afternoons made it dat knife-handle." We keep it yet in memory of Sebattis. Alone, all alone in the woods, he was respecting his conscientious scruples about Sabbath-keeping.

It was when he was out among people that his moral nature was not equal to the strain. The sins of this world were so attractive to him. Once he was arguing seriously against paying his honest debts. He had planned a great and varied round of pleasures, the full circle of a white man's debauch, with all the buggy-riding he wanted. " We sorry we cahn' paid you; we owed it an' we ought paid it an' we got money, but we was goin' get drunk jus' like white man an' have hell of good time, an' you see dose t'ings she 's berry 'spensive." This time he squandered his money strictly according to the programme, but at other times he was not so successful. His love of fair play was a great disadvantage to him. After he had planned some sharp bit of knavishness, for fear he might not be quite fair about it, he would very likely go and explain to his unsuspecting victim his whole intentions and show just how and when he could best be outwitted. If his friendly offices against himself were accepted and his game was blocked, then apparently no one was so much pleased about it as Sebattis. " Well, you was *smart!* We did n't t'ought you 'd got it your money; but you was *smart!* "

But one point he never failed in, and

that was in fidelity to his work. I have known him to stay three weeks at the stupid task of watching a dam, though he had nothing to eat but spoiled pork and flour, and he knew that all the other boys were off having fun on the logs. He was with all his heart and soul wrapped up in the welfare of the West Branch Drive, and he would have broken all the commandments *seriatim* if that would have helped the logs along. Captain Hilton of Chesuncook, between laughter and vexation, was telling once how Sebat came along "playing big Injun," with a crowd of fellows tagging after to do his commands, and how he cleaned up the 'Suncook shores in the interest of P. L. D. "After he was gone along, you could n't find a paddle nor a peavey anywhere, unless it was under lock and key. He could n't read the marks on them, and he had to keep up his dignity, so he took no chances. 'She looks like P. L. D.; best way you took him, boys.' He even carried off my big boom anchor that weighed three hundred. 'Dat anchor, she look like P. L. D.; best way you took him.' P. L. D. never lost anything by Sebattis."

Nor could his other employers have been greatly dissatisfied. Mr. Dillingham, the Indian agent, said years ago that Sebat was trusted more than any other Indian that he ever knew. Lumbermen would let him go into the woods in the fall, explore his own berth of timber, locate his camp and hovels, build the same, take the whole charge of some thirty men and ten or a dozen horses, and bring his brook-drive down to the main drive, without having a white man go near him except to settle with the men. Judged by this, there must have been some ground for Sebat's sharp distinction between a man who is drunken and a competent man who drinks.

Sebat was quick to see a point. John Ross had a bad jam on at one time, too bad a jam to send men out upon against their wishes. "If you want to go out and break that jam, Sebat, there's a chance to get your name in the papers," said he.

Sebattis looked at him as sharp as a cock-sparrow. "What good do dead Injun get damn name in papers?" said he. He knew very well that between the police-court records and the funeral notices, there was no room in the papers for an Indian.

"Sebat," said one of his many employers, willing to do a good deed for the world, "you ought n't to swear so. Don't you know that you won't ever get to heaven if you swear like that?"

Sebat considered the proposition half a second, stopping his work to do so. "I tell you what, Jim; we goin' give him hard one!" Once more it was the Penobscot man, self-reliant and quite confident of arriving.

In this story of running Canaan Falls there is no sure evidence that Sebattis was the bowman of the boat; but another incident will show well enough that it could have been no other, — not while he was in the boat, as we know that he was. The story is delightfully Sebattis, too.

It was late in the Civil War, when men were in great demand, high bounties being offered to substitutes. One day a friend said, " Do you know a black little Indian who calls himself Sebattis Solomon ? "

"I should think I might," was the reply. " He has worked in my haying crew for three years now ; he enlisted only the other day and went straight off to war."

The other laughed. " Where do you suppose he got to? Not to the war at all, for he did n't enlist. I was in the provost-marshal's office the other day, and this fellow came in, as drunk as an owl, with a lumberman who had been drafted, and who offered him eight hundred dollars bounty to go in his place. He was in his shirt-sleeves, with a fig-drum on his head for a hat, and was marching around all ready to go to war; the job just suited him. He said his name was Sebattis Solomon."

" It certainly was ; that is Black Sebat."

" He marched up to the enlisting officer, and the first thing he said was : ' We want 'list. We want for 'list um colonel ! ' That was a pretty literal application of the principle of room near the top. They told him that they had no vacancies just then in that rank, but they could give him a good place a little lower down, with the rank of a full private. But he insisted on enlisting as a colonel. 'We want for 'list um *colonel!*' That was all that could be got out of him. He went off without enlisting at all."

Sebattis, it is plain, had a Penobscot man's opinion of his own capabilities. He knew that any man who could drive four white horses, or handle thirty Penobscot lumbermen, or take a drive down in the spring, was perfectly qualified to command a paltry thousand of counter-jumpers. No, sir! It was colonel or nothing! Not even that rank of full private and those eight hundred dollars — a large sum to a man who has holes in all his pockets — could break his determination to take nothing below his deserts. Therefore one has no hesitancy in saying that he was the bowman of that boat which ran Canaan Falls, because there would have been trouble if he had not been; nor that, even if the intention did not originate with him, as was most likely, he was the one who sanctioned it. It was like Sebattis Solomon to

have ideals which he held high and followed loyally, even though he got mired
sometimes in the muck of his daily life.

And so, through the return of the
river-drivers triumphant, their idealization
of John Ross, because he always led them
to victory, the dogged faithfulness and
fantastic pride of Black Sebat, we come
back to the Connecticut River again, to
Canaan Falls in the blithe June weather,
when a little farther down the river, however it may be there, the laurel is white
as snow on the hillsides, and the thrasher
sings and the wood-thrush, and the scarlet
tanager flashes a living coal among the
green of the chestnut-trees.

I never saw the place, know nothing of
it, save as these men told the story, and
repeat that only from the memory of many
years back; but if it was as they said,
Canaan Falls was a rapid which had never
been run within the memory of man. All
were agreed that it was impossible water.
Just above the falls, where the full summer
strength of the great river was rushing
down, a bridge crossed, a bridge with stone

piers. Behind each pier played an eddy, and on the lower side of one was a ring-bolt drilled into the rock. John Ross's drive was down as far as Hanover, and one boat's crew waited behind this pier while two of the men went uptown on an errand. There were four Indians in the boat, — Sebattis Solomon, Mitchell Soc Francis, Sappiel Orson, and Sebattis Clos-sian. Three out of the four had been drinking, though which was the fourth may be left to their intimate friends to de-termine; it could not have been Sebattis Solomon, because he would have resented the imputation of sobriety quite as quickly as he did its opposite.

It was snug and comfortable there, and they gathered in the middle of the boat and stretched out their big spike-boots; perhaps, if the errand was a long one and the boat dry, they curled down crosswise amidships, reclining against her flaring sides, smoking and whittling. There they sat, hats pulled down or pushed back, — for who ever saw a river-driver without his hat at one extreme or the other? —

and laughed and chatted in Indian, gos-
siping, as Indians love to do, over the
long-winded nothings which they spin out
so attractively. It was fine June weather,
the drive was all right; no thought now
of those great meadows in Massachu-
setts where the current eats in under one
bank, leaving the other high and dry, nor
of the river's tortuous windings, nor the
Ox-bow, nor the strong water at Titan's
Pier, nor the falls at Holyoke, nor the
shallows below the falls; they did not
know the river and the "grief" ahead of
them; they lay and chatted like the bob-
olinks that sang above them in the grassy
banks. Every now and then a step
sounded on the planking of the bridge;
perhaps a shaking of dust came sifting
down and was filtered in a band of sunlight, — men's steps, sharp and quick;
women's steps, short and fussy; children's
steps, uneven, joyously eager, or loiter-
ing by turns, as they paused or hastened,
fancy-struck. Not all of the steps passed.
Those who stopped to look over the rail
saw beneath the queer sharp-ended boat

and the four black, rough-looking men, talking a strange, soft language with liquid gutturals and pretty circumflexes; they saw them whittling in a strange way with a strange-looking knife, drawing it toward them with great precision, and they saw them also passing from hand to hand a flat black bottle. The men were drinking quietly, not enough to incapacitate them, — which, as Sebattis said, "can't be done." These men were doing nothing which they considered reprehensible, and one of them never drank. There was some joke on hand about the bottle just then. Sebattis Solomon had looked into it last, a little too long, perhaps, for the next man, holding it up to the light, shook it gently, as if to make more of what was in it. And he murmured ruefully in English, "Seems like them whiskey she's thunderin' few!" Then he passed the empty flask to the man who did not drink, who threw it into the river, and they all laughed softly. They were having as good a time as a family of muskrats before the white folks disturbed them.

For the feet up on the bridge kept up their rap-tap-tap. More and more of them came, and they kept stopping. Few passed, it would seem; for, looking up, one saw a line of faces looking down, straight down upon that boat.

The Indians talked to each other in Indian, commenting upon the number of people who were curious to look at an Indian, as if his place was in a show, and they chaffed Sebattis Solomon as being fit for the part of the monkey, turning an organ-crank in pantomime and pulling an imaginary string; Sebat was the butt of all sorts of witticisms.

Then a woman's high voice said, " Ask them, why don't you?" They heard that.

Then a man hailed them. " What time are you going to run these falls?"

"Ugh-hugh!" said Black Sebat sharply, turning to the next man and repeating it in Indian as if the man could not understand English. " He says, ' What time are you going to run these falls?' All these people are waiting to see us run these falls."

No direct answer did he make to his

questioner on the bridge, which was an Indian trait; but there began an animated jabber among themselves in their own tongue. It was the first notion that any of them had of running Canaan Falls; for everybody who knew about water knew that the place could not be run. Some foolish loiterer, seeing the boat holding there, and perhaps not even knowing that an eddy is a good place to wait in, nor how many men make a boat's crew, nor that watermen do not commonly risk their lives for the pleasure of people who know nothing about logs and water, not caring overmuch for their approval, had started the rumor that the Indians were going to run the falls. And already upon the end of the bridge fell the sharp pat of running feet coming to see the Indians act in the melodrama of running Canaan Falls.

It was not that which moved them to do it; there was nothing of the purely spectacular about it; Joe Orson, when he told the story, revealed that clearly enough, for, though at the time he told it he thought it was himself instead of his brother who was in the boat, all the more did what he say demonstrate, by its avowal of his willingness to have done the same, and his approval of what was done, that a perfectly pure and lofty motive impelled them to the act.

Perhaps the one sober man tried to dissuade them ; for he would see that the foolish report of foolish idlers did not bind men to risk their lives. But the ideas of the others were just enough out of focus to make them loom grandly ; prudence did not preach to them half so loud as it would have done an hour before. They saw larger relations, grander achievements, the ideal beckoning them ; they felt the pressure of moral obligation. It is a stage that comes to an Indian in this condition with remarkable regularity of recurrence. He needs just that stimulus to bring all his powers out of a dual and antagonistic relation into harmonious working ; for he is not one man, but two — a white man and an Indian, and only the finest and the strongest among them can bridge that gulf by their own wills.

So they talked rapidly, gesturing and arguing. Then Sebattis Solomon stood up in the stern and picked out a course. Then, while the others found their places, he ran forward to the bow, cast off the painter from the ring-bolt, and swung her to the stream. So they went down into the white of Canaan Falls.

How they fared I cannot even imagine, not knowing the place. What sort of water it was, too deep, too scanty, too rocky, too beset with heaving boils, they never told me. We had few watermen their equals, yet they could not make the run. The boat swamped and was wrecked. The men were thrown out into the swirl and rush of the water and carried down among rocks and white boils into the race of the rapids below. Three were saved, Sebattis Solomon being pulled in by a man who ran out and reached a pick-pole to him as he was being swept past; he grasped the extreme tip of it, but such was the grip of his horny fingers that he held with one hand in all that current and was drawn out safe. The man who had the best chance of all, who had won through to safety, and was resting in the eddy behind a pier of logs below the fall, in attempting to break through the current and swim ashore, was caught by the undertow and drowned.

Joe Orson told the story in the saloon of the old Cambridge, steaming home from their great Connecticut River Drive, his eyes very bright, his whisper most impressively aspirate. He was himself in just the condition to see things large, and no doubt he interpreted all more truly and even more dramatically for the slight mistake of not being able to tell whether he was himself or his brother. It held a noble pathos, too. This was no crack-brained, dare-devil feat, but an act of the highest devotion.

"You see we had to go. There was younk man, old man, boy, gal, all sorts was lookin' right down on *us*. Oldtown Injun she got great name for ribber-dribin'. We mus' go. We knew it was *die* that time, but we must n' go back on our name!"

"Both sweet and becoming it is to lay down one's life for one's country," sings

the stately Roman poet. Four Penobscot
Indians, men who have no country, in the
face of dangers which they fully compre-
hend, cheerfully elect to die for the honor
of the tribe; and the man who told it
would have done the same; and all the
others who were there approved it and
would have done the same. The honor
of the tribe, the fame of the West Branch
Drive, the reputation of the Penobscot
man, were the ideals that beckoned them.

Oh, the folly of all self-sacrifice, the
vanity of all things beautiful, the lying
promise of spiritual ends which the cynic
preaches! "This might have been sold
for much and given to the poor!" Verily.
Yet when the poor had eaten and drunken
it, what then? But the precious waste-
fulness, preserved within a book, — how
many are fed from the ambrosia of such a
fair and noble deed!

"But they were drunk when they did
it," cry the modern disciples, indignant at
seeing the virtue of sobriety infracted, "and
that takes away the merit of the act." Yet
remember that the thoughts which came

then to them were but the reflexes and enlargements of the thoughts which filled their sober hours, not something new and unaccustomed, but what they commonly concealed, and perhaps could not act out with full volition. Prudence might have prevented the actual doing of the deed, dumbness might have tied Joe Orson's tongue in telling of it, had they been strictly temperate; but in all the thought would have been there, the impulse would have been there, the binding force of pride, the pure ideal of an honorable sacrifice, would still have been a motive working latently, even though we had never seen it as an active force.

What drives logs to market? Stout muscle; strong will; pure sentiment. Even here the Ideal has its place.

The gamesters and loiterers about the hotels in Hartford were laying bets, five to one, that that fellow from the Penobscot would lose his whole drive. A very quiet stranger in brown was going about taking up small amounts.

"Are you a stranger here?" asked a good-natured man; "well, then, take a friend's advice and don't bet against a sure thing; we have lived on this river some time, and that drive's hung up, a dead loss."

Still the quiet stranger kept right on taking up small amounts.

A week later came the word that the drive was safe, down to Springfield, where it could be towed the rest of the way. Then the stranger went around settling bills that brought him in five to one.

"I hate to take money on a sure thing like this," said he apologetically.

A loser hissed, "Cheat! You knew it! You knew what we did n't."

The stranger looked at him; he melted, — it was a hot day.

"I guess I *did* know what you did n't," said he very quietly. "I 've seen the West Branch Drive before — I 'm Penobscot myself — and I know John Ross."

But there are no such unsatisfactory people in the world to talk to as the fine and finicky folk who refuse to see by any light but the fox-fire of their own prejudices. The man behind the palm-leaf fan was fast asleep.

IX

RESCUE

RESCUE

A FORGOTTEN story, a nameless hero.

Who the man was no one knows, except
that he was a Spencer. This in no way
distinguishes him; it is but saying, in other
words, that he was a riverman, and begs
the question of his identity, the Spencers
being not a family, but a tribe. We might
guess that his name was Elijah, and guess
aright most likely; but this is nothing by
which he could be discriminated, for every
Spencer who was not named something else
was named Elijah.

What sort of a Spencer was he? That
is just what the story refuses to tell us:
good or bad; honest or knavish; lettered
or illiterate; a sober, thrifty, useful citi-
zen, or the most worthless ever spawned
in Argyle, all that we know for a certainty
is that he had in him the right stuff of
heroes. For out of all the rescues that I
ever heard of, this is the one which had in

it the least of bravado and the most of determined courage, the one which the man who started out to make it might have given up with good excuse at any point, and yet that he seems never to have thought of giving up for a moment, but fought through in the face of incredible obstacles.

His reward? To be forgotten so entirely that no one knows his name. Almost is the deed itself passed out of memory. I heard it fifteen years ago from Reed McPheters, when we were encamped close by where it happened, and in all the years since, asking this one and that one who has spent his life upon the river, I found no one who knew the tale. It sounded all straight, they said, but they had never heard of it, and there were so many Spencers; they could n't guess which one this was. I despaired of ever learning more, when at last I was directed to the brother of one of the men engaged. He certified to the main points and added new details. This is the story, built up from both accounts; it may be accepted as not far from the facts.

It happened up near Fowler's Carry, where now is the city of Millinocket. Whose wildest dreams ten years ago would ever have fabled a modern city springing up within the fastnesses of that forest? For more than sixty years, the only house between Little Schoodic and Chesuncook had been the Fowler homestead on the lower end of the carry. There or near by there, for fifty-four years, up to the year 1884, when they sold it to Charley Powers, who in turn sold the land to build a city on, no one but Fowlers had ever lived on Fowler's Carry. They were pioneers among a race of pioneers and watermen of superlative excellence. It did not hurt the pride of any man to hear it said that, between the Lower Lakes and Medway, the Fowler boys could do on the river what no other men dared to do. Everybody was free to admit that much. " Those Fowler boys," as Mrs. McCauslin said to Thoreau so long ago as 1846, " are perfect ducks for the water." As well they might be, brought up in the woods with no neighbors within miles, and never a highroad except in winter but such as was afforded by a wild and frothing river, rushing down over endless rapids and falls.

At the time of this story, the two brothers Frank and John Fowler, with their families, were living in the old homestead on the carry. To understand at all this story, it is needful to bear in mind the lay of the land; for this man Spencer had to swing around a circle of not less than nine miles before he could accomplish what he started out to do, namely to rescue four men who were in great peril on the Gray Rock of Island Falls. The difficulty is that Fowler's, unlike all the other carries of the West Branch, does not skirt the river-bank, but is, or was, a cross-country road from water to water, cutting off a great bend in the river. To one looking up the river from the Forks at Medway, it is as if he held a sickle left-handed, with his thumb stuck straight out where he grasped the handle. At the tip of the blade, like a plum upon the point of the sickle, would be Quakish Lake; the curving steel would be the West Branch of the Penobscot, tear-

ing down a rocky course, some hundred
and fifty feet of fall in about four miles;
the handle, with the knuckles around it,
would be Shad Pond, and the outstretched
thumb would be Millinocket Stream coming in from the north. Now Fowler's Carry
ran from a point about two miles up Millinocket Stream to a point about a fourth
of a mile below Quakish Lake at the tip
of the sickle. The carry was called two
miles long, which in Maine always means
abundant measure, and yet it was a far
shorter portage than would have been required in following the river with all its
falls: first, as one leaves Quakish, Rhine's
Pitch of about ten feet; then Island Falls
of two miles of very strong water with a
heavy fall,—twenty feet in twenty rods in
one place, — and Grand Falls, a mile long,
with the Grand Pitch, twenty feet perpendicular, just before the river enters Shad
Pond. Fowler's, undoubtedly chosen by
the Indians ages ago as the shortest and best
route from lake to lake, did not go near the
river; in most places it was from two to
more than three miles away from the river.

It was the very last day of April, 1867, when Scott and Rollins turned out their logs from the boom on Quakish Lake. Theirs was not the main West Branch Drive, but a private drive, which got into Quakish much earlier and was worked along by a single boat's crew of seven men. That is why no one knows about the matter; for if the success of a jest lies in the ear of the hearer, much more does the memory of a heroic deed depend upon the eye of the spectator. But in this case had there been on-lookers, they never would have permitted Spencer to do what he did; they would have insisted upon helping, and so would have spoiled the story.

The last of April — seven men working on the logs at Quakish, one of them a Spencer. One who knows the place and the season has to stop and think about what it brings back to him, — crisp air; freezing nights; snowdrifts in the shaded hollows, and patches of dark ice, covered with hemlock needles, among the black growth; the chittering of red squirrels chasing each other and the pleasant con-

versation of chickadees consulting where
to dig their nest. The round-leaved yellow violet is out then, even so far north as
that, and the brown-winged *Vanessa* butterfly. How they endure the freezing nights
no one knows, but for weeks now, fuzzy
black-ended brown caterpillars have been
crawling around on the snow. The bees
are nosing about the woodpiles, their
heads close to the sappy ends of the
sticks, and the little flies that dance like
tiny sprites in the golden light of sunset
are treading up and down on air in their
bewildering mazes. Out in the fields the
sheep sniff the earth, and the cattle bite
it for a relish; the ploughed land lies in
furrows, wet and rank to the nostril, a
wholesome smell — for one must remember again that spring comes late to these
northern clearings. Leaves there would
be none upon the hard wood; but the red
maple might be blossomed like coral and
the poplar beginning to fringe itself with
silvery tassels, while birch and alder showed
their corded catkins of twisted bullion and
the " pussies " on the willows were large

enough fairly to be called "cats," and were alive with bees. The squaw-bush [1] would have lost something of the scarlet lacquer of its stems, and the big marsh willows would be less golden in their twigs. Already the partridges would have quit their diet of birch and poplar buds and be feeding on the shrubby willows in the lowlands, or foraging for the green leaves of last year's clover and goldthread. Already the fish-hawk would be at work at Shad Pond, carrying sticks to repair his family homestead, while up at Quakish, his natural enemy and bully, the great bald eagle, might be whiling away his idle time in honest fishing from his old station on a boomstick.

One never knows the idyllic charm of our northern woods who has not seen them in April, when it is all a feast of birds and buds and waking life. Midsummer does not compare with this. This month belongs to the birds and flowers ; but most of all to the robin. I cannot tell this story

[1] A local name for the *Cornus stolonifera*, red-osier dogwood.

without giving the robins the place which I know they must have had in it, — great husky fellows, as red as blood in the lifting between showers that made a golden sunset, sitting high in the treetops and splitting their throats with their rain-carol, singing in jubilance at being back again, glad to find once more the corner of the earth that they were born in, and trolling forth such lusty music that all their pertness and swagger and pilfering of a later date is forgiven in advance. Of all the birds of springtime, I would like best to be the robin just getting back to his old home; for it is brave and blithe and bonny that he is, and he is April to all of us in the far north.

So here there must have been robins, cheerful in the face of all weathers, singing their best when the skies are lowering and the mist drives down the lake. For whatever may be the joys of April at its loveliest, it would seem that this was a bad one. There are evidences in the story that much rain had fallen and was still falling, else why such a rapid rise of water after the most of the snow was gone and the river should have been quieting down to the ordinary driving-pitch? Quakish, then, instead of a sapphire lake girdled with the green of spruces, must have been gray and mist-enshrouded, the nights warmer than on fairer days, and the days alternations of misty sunshine and smart showers of finely sifted rain, — a whole week of wet weather that melted the snows in the woods, that overfilled the bogs, that left all the mosses green and spongy, overflowing in little streams which trickled down all the tiny runlets, and that dripped from the mossy cedars leaning out over Quakish, funereally draped in gray-green moss, — good weather enough for robins, who love the wet, but not such good weather for men driving logs.

The trouble, so Reed said, was in turning the logs out of the boom in Quakish too early. Just what that means is doubtful, if it does not imply long-continued rain, which would swell the river rapidly and make the work of driving the logs more difficult and dangerous than ordinary. Whatever it means, the very first thing, they got a jam on the old Gray Rock just below

Rhine's Pitch and about a quarter of a mile above the head of Island Falls. It was a middle-jam, which is the worst to pick, and they had only a single boat's crew to take care of it. Scott, who was one of the head men of that drive, went down to Fowler's at the lower end of the carry at once, and offered the two brothers, John and Frank, fifteen dollars a day to go up and handle boats and do general work. That was the first day of May, and that very day Frank Fowler had gone up to Big Smith Brook to work for Fowler and Lynch. We hear no more of Scott in this story; it seems likely that, without going back to his men at all, he hastened out to Medway, twelve miles away, to pick up a crew there, and that he did not get back again till the story was over.

Meantime there were but seven men to look after that jam and whatever logs of theirs were running free. They had but their one boat, which it would never do to risk, and so they must have worked short-handed, some on the jam, the rest along the shore keeping the boat by them, ready to rescue the others if anything happened. The water must have been terribly rough then, and one who knows what to listen for in imagination can hear the hiss of the great boils and the bursting of the bubbles in the long white foam-streaks striping the waves which went rushing past, running deep and wicked. Out there in the scuds of rain, one who knows what to see can see once more the piled-up middle-jam and the four men upon it, red shirts and peavies, pulling and prying and pushing to loosen one by one the great jackstraws under their feet and send them darting down the rushing river, — precarious work, this, to pry out the foundations under your feet when you know that there is nothing beneath but water running at a race-horse rate, and below, two miles of dangerous falls.

How long the men had been working on that jam, why Spencer and the others started to take them off, at what time of day the catastrophe happened, neither account satisfactorily determines. Reed understood that the jam hauled suddenly,

and left only about twenty logs upon the
rock, with the four men on them. Frank
Fowler, who should know if any man does,
says otherwise, that the jam did not start
till some time in the night. Even without
the authority of his statement, this would
be the better reason; for the former situation is too thrilling by half for a real
event, and instead of urging Spencer on to
such desperate efforts would, by making
it hopeless from the start, have left him
nothing to labor for. It seems most prob-
able that the larger half of the crew had
been working on this jam since Scott left
them the day before (for it is now the
second day of May, 1867), the other three
resting or working near the boat, to be
ready in case of accident; that the time
must have been not far from six o'clock,
the old-fashioned sun-time, which came a
half hour later by the light than the railroad standard of to-day; and that it was
now approaching supper-time, and the boat
was coming out to take the men off. For
it could not have been dark enough to quit
work at that season, even of a lowery or a

rainy day ; but the river-driver's supper hour is seven o'clock, and as these were but a single boat's crew, too few men to carry a cook and separate wangan, they must leave the logs long enough before dark to cook for themselves. It seems likely that it was, as the men would say, "just about half-past hungry time," and the men on the jam saw with pleasure the boat, with Spaulding, Moores, and Spencer in it, dropping down to take them off. Perhaps the rain held up a little and the yellow of the sunset behind the rain-cloud showed through it, and the robins in the treetops all along the shore were singing, to be seen but not to be heard above the tumult of the water.

" Pretty birds them be to sing," the men might have remarked, leaning on their peavies, " and awful nice in pies." It may sound materialistic, but why is it not better that a robin should be good in a pie as well as out of it? They were willing enough to give him credit for his music, but supper was what was in their thoughts. And here were Spaulding and Moores and Spencer letting the boat down, two with their poles, one at the oars, intending to drop her into the eddy below the jam. Then the four men would tumble in, three of them would take an oar apiece, the boy would sit aft on the lazy seat, and back they would go to camp-fire, supper, and bed.

Two of those men were doomed to make their bed in a different place that night; and but for a miracle, the like of which I never heard of happening, all seven of them would have been there before morning.

It was but a step more to safety in the eddy, when snap went the stern-pole, and around the boat swung broadside to the current. Before they could straighten her with paddles she was swept down upon the head of Island Falls. She struck a rock, cracked open, and overset, all in the same instant. Quick? A driving-boat is *built* to act quick; that is her special virtue.

There were now three men and a wrecked boat in the water of Island Falls, and four men on a jam in the middle of the river,

powerless to save them. If the initial disaster was quick, the final one was to the
spectators a prolonged agony. Two of
their mates they saw drowned outright,
and for the third there was no hope. There
were they, four wet, hungry, shivering
men, a moment before so near to blankets, supper, and fire, now abjectly miserable on a log-jam in mid-river, no one
knowing of their plight, rain falling, night
coming fast, the river rising, the jam they
were on already beginning to feel the
freshet and grow uneasy, their own danger
imminent, and their hearts wrung by seeing
a catastrophe which they could have in no
wise prevented. They were hungry, cold,
wet, miserable, disheartened men, in peril
of their lives. Did the robin still sing
in the treetops? Then they damned his
unseemly levity, and in the same breath
wished they had the pie he was made for.

Two men were drowned outright, and
so have nothing further to do with the
story. No doubt they were as good men
as any of those saved, as good watermen,

perhaps, as Spencer was ; but it was their
fate to lose their lives, not to give them
away. Moores was found about a month
later down at Jerry Brook, and there was
buried. Spaulding was not discovered till
some time in September, under a log
where the old mill-pond was, down at Medway, sixteen miles below where he was
drowned. 'T is only a sample of what all
river-stories are like ; in almost all some
one loses his life, and no one thinks of
him afterward except the family, that sets
one less chair at table, and a few mates
here and there, who date their stories by
the year such and such an one was
drowned.

Meantime Spencer, on whom everything depends, is at the mercy of a raging
flood on the head of Island Falls. There
are two miles of this tumultuous water,
but the River helped him. All watermen
know — indeed, any one may observe the
same thing by watching even a gutter-
current — that all swift water has a pulse-
beat ; nominally its waves are stationary,

but every now and then there comes a
larger one, swelling quick and high with
a sudden throb, quite different from the
ordinary stationary wave. No sooner had
Spencer been thrown into the water than
one of these great waves took him and
lifted him fairly up on the bottom of his
overturned boat. It was slippery with wet
pitch; it was narrow; it had no keel; he
could not have held on at all, bucking and
rearing as it did, reeling and rocking, as
its long points, bow and stern, ploughed
under the great boils, had not the boat
when she turned over hit a rock so hard
as to split one side open. He got his
fingers into the crack, and it nipped them
there.

We have four men on a middle-jam
waiting to be drowned, two below drowned
already, and the seventh man with his
fingers caught fast in the crack in a crazy
old boat that — upside down, banging into
him, overriding him, slatting him against
rocks and logs, half drowned with spray
and rushing waters, half stunned with
being beaten against boat and rocks, his

fingers crushed and aching cruelly —
towed him the whole two miles down
Island Falls. "And if that wa'n't something of an experunce, then I don't never
want to have one happen to me!" says
the woodsman, who can appreciate better
than any amateur what it must mean.

It takes a good deal to drown a Spencer.
There is a story current about four Spencers and four Province men, a Mattawamkeag crew, going out in 1870 to pick
a jam on the upper pitch of Piscataquis
Falls. When they saw how bad the water
was, two of the Spencers leaped out of
the boat and got ashore again; the other
two Spencers and the Province men were
carried over the falls. The Spencers were
all right in the water, of course ; they expected to arrive somewhere. Old Lute
swam ashore about half a mile below, with
his T. D. pipe still in his teeth. He
emerged like Neptune, and shook the
water off all ready for some more river-
driving. Some bystander, a little curious,
inquired where he had come from. He
answered that he was " right down from

Piscataquis Upper Pitch, and he guessed
them four Bluenoses that was in the boat
with him was all drownded by that time!"
He was right, too. The Spencer whom
he did not worry about got ashore on the
boat.

This Spencer was dragged down through
Island Falls. Just as he reached the point
where he did not care to travel much farther
because below were the Grand Falls and
Grand Pitch, which nothing can go over
and live, the boat struck a wing-jam so
hard that the crack gaped and let his fingers out. Then the boat went off and left
him; for all this time the boat had been
holding him rather than he holding the
boat. As he was being carried past the
jam, he threw one arm over a log, and another of those great pulse-beats of the river
came, as before, and lifted him clear up
upon the jam. Reed had heard that at just
this moment the jam hauled, that he fell
in between the logs as they were moving,
grasped two of them, threw himself out
upon them, and ran ashore over the tum-
bling, moving mass. This is requiring too

much breath for even a Spencer. Any man, after being dragged through Island Falls the way this one had been, ought to have been grateful enough for the help of that great wave to lie there on the logs, sick and giddy and aching, till he got the water out of him and the woods stopped spinning around him, the noise of the river became a less deafening roar, and he could see the trees and logs in their natural color instead of just the black shapes of logs and trees.

It was getting quite dusk beneath the trees, and here was he, a battered and disabled man, alone on the river-bank, two miles below his comrades in distress and four miles at least from Fowler's, nothing for him to do but to get his legs under him and limp along the best he could to Fowler's Carry. John and Frank would go up and take the men off, and all would come out right.

The water was very strong; it was rising fast; to lose a moment would not do, for no one could tell how soon, under such a pressure as that, the jam on the Gray Rock might give way. He scrambled up, hobbling painfully, perhaps putting his fingers to his mouth to ease them, for they were raw and bloody and still white at the ends from the pinching they had received in the old boat's side; the split board working back and forth had maimed them cruelly. Then he set off down the drivers' path past Grand Falls. There was a boat down below the Grand Pitch, and it was easier, if not shorter, to go by water than to go through the woods, if, indeed he was landed on the left bank at all, which the story does not say. He walked and he ran and he hurried hobbling for a mile, when he reached the place where the boat was. Then he rowed down Shad Pond for a mile, and then poled up Millinocket Stream for two miles more. It must have taken him an hour at least since he was washed ashore below Island Falls, and it was now on the edge of darkness, the time when the robins are flying with sharp *peeps* and *queeps*, jetting their tails and talking about going to bed, for the robin is rather late about his hour of retiring.

At Fowler's landing Spencer hauled his boat up ashore enough to hold her, and then toiled up the hill to the house. He was very much done out. However, he could get the Fowler boys to go over with their boat, and he would have no more worries. He was hungry, too. A woodsman's appetite is not a fickle fancy for victuals, to be lost or forgotten just because he has had some strain upon his nerves. Perhaps, as he dragged himself wearily up the hill in the dusk, he smelled that most appetizing of all the smells of springtime, the odor of smoked alewives roasting before an open fire. He could see in fancy the row of golden-sided fishes, standing on their heads before the bed of coals, as they leaned against the tongs laid across the fire-dogs and gave forth, when they cracked open, a smell so savory that no one who cannot remember smelling it in damp April weather can dream how good it is. Spencer quickened his steps, always supposing that he actually did smell it, for, where the story is silent, conjecture has the right to wander.

He went up to the log-house, finished within and without with rifted cedar, and appeared before the women within like an apparition. It was long after supper; they were finishing the last of the supper-dishes, and the delicious odor was only from the refuse of the feast smouldering upon the coals. He was disappointed, more so than he would have cared to own. He had been planning on being asked to supper, and had anticipated his enjoyment of his share.

"Where's John and Frank?" he asked abruptly, stopping in the doorway, a big, black bulk in the gloaming.

"Lord! how you scared me!" cried one of the women.

"Did n't mean to, mum," was his weak apology, leaning against the door-jamb; he knew that he was faint as well as hungry. "Where's John and Frank?"

"Milking," said John's wife.

"Up Big Smith Brook; went up yesterday," said Frank's wife, each one answering for her own.

He dropped into a seat with a groan.

"Why, what's the matter?" asked one

of the women kindly. " You do look all beat out! No hat, and — land sakes! you're wet to the skin! Here, draw up close to the fire and get het up. What have you been doing of?"

Whether she had ever seen him before made no difference, the cordiality of those pioneer homes being too real for any formality. She drew him up to the fire and bade him rest. "What's the matter now?" she asked. There was always something the matter on those falls.

" Just ben runnin' Island Falls on the bottom of a boat," said he. His fingers almost made him wince when he got them near the fire.

She was a pioneer woman, and could think and act promptly. " Here, Billy and Ann," — or whatever were the names of the first children she could catch, — "just you run out to the barn and tell your father to come right in; there's been a boat swamped up on Island Falls."

" What become of the others?" she asked, turning to the man.

He did not like to say it too bluntly.

" They 're where they won't get out till they are taken out, I guess, mum," he answered.

She stood and plaited the hem of her apron. " How many ? " she asked.

" Two — there was three of us in the boat. The other four 's out on the jam on the old Gray Rock, if so be she ain't hauled yet."

The other woman had stood silent beside her sister-in-law. " And only you and John to do it; and you so used up! How can you ever ? "

" Got to," said he.

There is never any fun in being a hero. This man did n't look the hero either, just a worn-out, tired, used-up man, with hair all tossed and tangled, a stoop in his shoulders, a crook in his back, and every rag upon him steaming before the fire. His hands he held down between his knees; he did not wish to have the ladies see them; they were not presentable.

These were women who knew what to do for a man. Already one of them had poured hot water on fresh tea leaves, while the other stooped and stood a herring up against the andiron bar, close to the coals.

"You ought not to, mum," said the man; "I ain't got time to eat; we've got to git right off; there ain't no time to eat." It was a feeble remonstrance. He wanted that alewife; the sight of it put more heart into him than anything else could have done, and to sit and sip his tea and watch that broil would, he felt, make a new man of him.

"You've got plenty enough time to eat," said one of the sisters-in-law, both hospitably busy with laying plates and tea-things and bringing out the food in store. "It's too bad you are too late for regular supper; things don't taste so good cold, but we'll warm up the biscuit, if you don't mind them a little crusty." No doubt the table was spread with other seasonable food: cold buckwheat cakes, perhaps, with the richest and sweetest of maple syrup, made from their own trees, and spicy dried-apple sauce, as brown as mahogany, fla-vored with nutmeg and dried orange peel, a delicious spring dainty, or custard pie without stint of eggs, and thick, soft gingerbread, such as woodsmen love best of anything,—"the odds and ends," as no doubt the ladies said, but food enough and good enough for any one; for these frontier homes were places where there was no lack of good fare, and where no one was allowed to pass without the invitation to partake it.

"Just you rest easy," said the sisters, caring for him. "John has got the boat to see to, and to get the drag down to it, and to yoke up the oxen. You can't help a bit more than the children can till it comes to getting the boat on; then maybe it will take the whole of us, she's so big and heavy. You wait till you are called for and get rested; you'll need all the strength you've got when the time comes." So well did they perform their part, that before the boat was ready he was fit to do his share in helping John Fowler.

Meantime John Fowler was losing no minutes. He understood what his wife meant when he had come in with the foaming milk-pails and she had laid her hand upon his arm. It was: "*Must* you go,

John?"—not dissuasion, but wifely concern.

All he said—for he knew that it meant some desperate undertaking—was, "How many? Where are they?"

A rescue is an obligation on all rivermen. While a chance remains it is not to be given up, no matter what it costs. "Drown ten men to save two," is the unwritten code of the River. The way in which this has been lived up to is one of the explanations of the willingness of the men to go into all sorts of hard places: they know that if human skill can do it, they are to be saved. Once when two men were adrift on the logs at Piscataquis Lower Pitch, six boats' crews, thirty-six men in all, leaped into their boats and ran the falls to save those two. It was mad folly for them to do it all at once, for the water was terribly rough; but they did it. Sebattis Solomon, good waterman as he was, almost lost his life in the attempt; for a leaping log knocked him out of his place in the bow, and had he not come up like a cork and thrown himself into his boat before his own midshipmen knew that he was out of it, he would not have lived to perform more deeds of water-craft.

This rescue on Island Falls was one of peculiar difficulty; for it must be made long after dark, in the worst of water, with only two men to handle a great Maynard boat whose crew should have been six men, four at the least. It required the most careful preparation for all emergencies. Everything must be provided at the outset. There were poles and paddles to be put into the boat, an axe, a rope, perhaps some dry kindling for starting big bonfires along the shores to light up the river; and there must be torches of birch-bark wound on slender poles to stick up in the boat, lighting more fully the track by which she traveled. Then the boat was too large and heavy for two men to launch, so rollers must be provided, that the pitch might not be scraped off on the rocks in getting her afloat. Then everything within the boat must be lashed in place, that on the rough trip across the carry nothing essential should be lost out. Finally, John Fowler

must get on his driving-boots and must
hitch up the cattle. Last of all, when the
drag was ready and Spencer stood beside it
with two of the children, one carrying a
lantern, it now being full dark, John Fowler had to go back again to get a little
bottle of matches, perhaps to say good-by
to his wife. To every one else those men
seemed the same as saved already because
he had started to do it, but he and she
might have felt the flutter of uncertainty.

So, with the children leading, to light the
road with the lantern, to tend the fires,
and, if accident were to be piled upon accident that day, as sometimes happens, to
bring back home the news of it, they set
off up the hill and across the rocky pas-
ture now growing up to pine bushes, with
the oxen going at as brisk a pace as was
good for either boat or cattle. Ahead
the children danced and trotted, their
swinging lantern a mere blur upon the
misty night. Then came the oxen on the
run, John Fowler giving them the gad,
while Spencer tried to keep the boat upright. The old drag smashed and bounced

on the great gray rocks embedded in the carry road, the boat was tossed more ways than if she were running the roughest water, and in spite of their lashings, the things inside her clattered and clashed. There was the jangling of chains, the shouting to the cattle, the creak of drag and boat, the rattle of the gad on horns and yoke, the racket of the poles inside the boat as they urged that cavalcade along, not sparing their speed. It was two miles to go, over as rough a road as a man cares to walk by daylight unencumbered, and then the off-set down to Rhine's Pitch. Half an hour? Well, if they did it in half an hour, that was quick time; the miles in that region are good measure, and the bounces and jounces are thrown in besides.

Meantime there had been four men sitting on a jam out in the middle of the river. Nothing more is known about them. Being merely dummies in the story, whose whole office was to permit themselves to be rescued, no one has thought to preserve their names. Nor would they

care themselves if we invent whom we will
to take their places.

There were, let us say, a boy of eighteen, off on his first drive, qualifying for the
West Branch ; an old soldier who would
have " seen her through," had not a minie
ball through the lungs mustered him out
at Gettysburg, — a lean, gaunt man, always
chirk and active, with a straggling, thin
beard, the type of many a veteran whom
we used to see when the war was over; and
there was Tom Smith of Oldtown, which
is no libel, for it used to be reported
of the Tom Smiths of Oldtown that they
named them Long Tom and Short Tom
and Chub Tom, and then they began and
numbered them, and they numbered them
up to sixteen. This one was Tom Smith
number sixteen and a half, the beginning
of a new series of Tom Smiths, and not
at all a bad sort of fellow ; he was probably dark, with curly hair, and having
been brought up in Oldtown, had never
believed that it was going to be his luck to
be drowned. The last was a short, thick-
set, swarthy man, part Inman, who sat

silent and smoked. He had nothing to say ; he did nothing ; he seemed to have no nerves ; but in a nook as well protected as any from the drive of the rain and the spray of the river, he sat with his hands in his pockets and pulled at his old pipe, facing death without the quickening of a pulse beat. That was partly because he was a man approaching middle-age, who had been on the river long enough to learn that if a man is born to be drowned, a mud-puddle in the road is deep enough to do it, and if he is n't born to be drowned, the whole Penobscot River cannot keep him under long enough to save him from his natural fate; so there is no use in worrying over what is going to happen to you, even if you do find yourself in a tight place. That is the philosophy of the River. All brave men are fatalistic ; the only objection to fatalism is when it is stupid.

But it is no comfortable situation to be where these men were, in a night of rain and mist, out on a pile of logs with the river rushing on all sides, so that it makes one giddy to see the white streaks racing

past, like looking out of a train window
in the dark at the lane of light which trav-
els beside it, — to be there without fire
or food or extra garments, and from hard
and heating labor suddenly to have to sit
down in a cold spring rain and wait for
hours, with nothing to think of but the
uncertainty of their fate and the horror
of what they had seen. The boy took it
hard; silently, of course, for stoicism is
the custom of the river, and no one here
likes to admit that he has any feelings; but
this was the first time he had ever seen
any one drown, and horror of it shook his
nerves, and made the night seem full of
noises; he was twice as chilly as he had
been, his teeth chattered, and he did not
like an old horned owl which kept hoot-
ing along the river-bank, audible above
the rushing of the water.

What had become of Spencer, they did
not know. They had seen him thrown up
on the boat by the great wave; he stood a
chance, that was all. If he were lost, they
were doomed. It was only a question of
time before that jam would be carried away

by the rising water. Tom Smith took out his pocket-knife, and reaching down among the logs, began cutting into the side of one. It was not dark then, only full dusk, and the rain had given way to mist.

"What doing, Tom?" asked the soldier.

"Getting spruce gum," replied Tom Smith.

But the man who asked the question was not deceived: one does not look for much spruce gum on a pine log; Tom Smith had been cutting a water-line where he could feel it after dark with his fingers, and judge by the rising of the water when that jam would haul. Then he shut his knife, and put it in his pocket.

"Find any gum, Tom?" inquired the ex-soldier.

"Nothin' good for anything," replied Tom Smith; "that log was all rossy [1] anyway." Then he went dumb again.

[1] *Rossy*, a very old word, used of shaggy-barked trees, chiefly of hard wood trees, like swamp maple; but sometimes also of scurfy or scaly barked soft woods. It applies only to the loose, outside bark, which is often called *ross*.

The ex-soldier understood the situation.
He had the boy on his mind, too; for he
had seen enough of raw recruits under
fire for the first time, and he did not
believe that it helps a man's after-career
to let his courage sink too low the first
time he is facing peril. One has to see
men die more or less, was his notion, and
the right thing to do is to think that it
is not at all unnatural: it does not follow
that one's own turn is coming next. He
began telling stories, funny stories, of times
when there was nothing to eat and some
one sneaked off with the best of the general's dinner, and his mess that day fared
all right; of times when in hard places
men were supremely comical and kept the
others laughing with their drollery; of
times when men did such great things
that only to hear of them was to applaud,
— stories like that of Major Hyde and
the Seventh at Antietam, and of Chamber-
lain at Little Round Top. He had been
— where had he not been? — at First
Bull Run, at Williamsburg, Chickahom-
iny, Fair Oaks, Antietam, Fredericksburg,

Chancellorsville, Gettysburg. At Gettysburg he saw — and then he stopped to cough.

" Quite a cough," said Tom Smith.

" Keeping that to remember Gettysburg by," replied the veteran, wiping his forehead; " sometimes when I 'm damp it comes on a little to 'mind me of old times."

It did not sound like a cough which river-driving would help to cure; but in that gaunt, thin-faced man with the straggling beard there was a power of grit. Just at present, instead of fretting because he could not get hot tea and warm blankets, he was taking upon himself to be the life of the little group upon the old Gray Rock.

" Oh, cheer up, sonny," said he to the boy; " don't you take it to heart so much; like 's not they are all snug somewheres; takes a deal of killing to use a man up, especially an able man at his trade. They 'll all come hypering back bime-by when they get 'em another boat; you would n't believe what a man can go through and not be hurt a bit; why, I knowed a man " —

Meantime Tom Smith was consulting his water-line.

"Gettin' some more of that same kind o' gum?" asked the soldier.

"Yes," said Smith gloomily. His line was half an inch under water in about an hour, he calculated. At that rate the jam could not hold together till morning. Three inches more, he reckoned, and she would haul. Already the water sobbed and chuckled higher among the timbers, and one of the big pulses of the river would send it spouting up through the chinks in the centre of the mass where before the water had been almost still. The jam lifted around the edges, too, when one of these big fellows came hurrying past. Of course there are plenty of youths who never saw anything but a millpond, who will be assured that, had they been there, they would just have caught hold of the biggest log they could find and have serenely floated down to safety: it would n't have worried them any, because they always can see easy ways out of sinking ships and burning buildings and dangers which they never experienced. To such a riverman would reply : " Our boys ain't onto them smart tricks o' yourn with logs, but when you try to l'arn us how, don't start in on a middle-jam on Island Falls." Tom Smith and the others who were used to the business saw nothing to do but to wait for the end of things right where they were.

" Just the same sort of gum as before ? " the old soldier had bantered, trying to get his information lightly.

" And it ain't no good sort, I can tell you," responded Tom Smith bitterly.

The old horned owl on the shore whooped again.

" Blame a owl ! " said Tom Smith.

The soldier kept right along with his story, " the awfuliest comical story that ever was about a man that got his head shot clean off ; something I seen myself."

His stories had more to do with sudden death than some would think in keeping with their surroundings ; but all tales of the river are tragic. These men did not mind mere tragedy. Under their environment, to talk of drowning would not have been etiquette, but there was something almost cheerful in hearing about a man to whom nothing worse happened than getting his head cut clean off with a cannon-ball.

The horned owl hooted again.

" Darn — a — *owl !* " said Tom Smith, in so ladylike a way that it took off all the objections to strong language. He had to say something. He did not like the hollow mockery of that great voice in the dark that cried, " Oh, who, who, who are you ? " He was n't going to be anybody by tomorrow morning, if Spencer had been drowned with the rest and that water kept on rising half an inch or more an hour ; he did not care to be reminded of the fact.

The ex-soldier coughed again, a racking spasm of coughing. River-driving in rainstorms and sitting out all night on middle-jams did not seem to be the sort of health-cure best adapted to a man who has had a minie ball through his lungs. Yet as soon as he could take his hands away from his side where he had pressed them, he began talking again, telling how he once made three men prisoners when he had nothing but an empty rifle; how when he was a vidette he used to trade tobacco with the enemy's outposts; how that first day at Gettysburg, the day before he got *this*, an old fellow in a high-crowned hat and a long-tailed blue had fought all day with the Seventh Wisconsin, and was a blame good shot, too; how at Yorktown, Old Seth of the Berdan Sharpshooters had captured one of the enemy's largest guns, and declared that if they would only bring him victuals enough, he could keep that gun till the end of the game, because not a man could get near to serve it while he had his bead on them. The man had seen life for three years, and there rose in him such a fountain of unquenchable vitality that no vicissitude nor danger could make him feel that he was not going to keep right on living; drown him on Island Falls if need be, and he would turn up somewhere else all alive and kicking, just as when they killed him in the army he had come out a river-driver. He did not worry about that cough even.

"Sometimes coughin' won't kill ye half so quick as ye wisht it would," was his cheerful philosophy.

"This old jam is heavin' now," cried the boy, clutching his arm.

"Don't ye be 'feared o' that, sonny," said he, as cool as ever; "you 've ben gettin' the water in your head, hearin' the rush of it so long; it 's just makin' you dizzy to see them white streaks racin' past; you 'll feel a big ram-dazzlefication when this here raft pulls off'n the old Gray. When I was sharpshootin' down in " —

The old horned owl hooted again sepulchrally and near: "Oh, who, who, who are you?"

"*Damn* a hoot-owl!" cried Tom Smith, not mincing matters. A loon and a hoot-owl were two birds which he had no use for, always glad to see a man get into trouble.

"And the mock-birds down south," went on the soldier, coughing worse, but bringing himself back to his self-imposed task, for he was intending to talk till the jam broke, just to keep that youngster's courage up — "and the mock-birds so sweetly singing " —

" Hist ! hark ! I hear 'em comin' ! " said the silent man. He had not spoken for almost two hours now.

They listened and could hear John Fowler shouting to his cattle ; then they saw the misty glow of the lantern ; then Spencer on the shore put his hands to his lips and gave a whoop that scared the hoot-owl out of competition.

Yes, they were all there.

That was good news, and it made the rescuers all the livelier at their work. It was not long before great fires were blazing on the shore, lighting the green wall of forest along the river-bank and the white scrolls of foam upon the water, and turning golden all the haze above the trees. The children fed them with dry brush from near at hand, and with every addition to the fires the blaze threw up an eruption of bright sparks and diffused an orange glare upon the blackness of the night. Then the great Maynard boat was rolled down to the water's edge and made ready, the blazing torch was stuck up in the peak of the bow, and, John Fowler in the bow, Spencer in the stern, they started to drop her down from the eddy below Rhine's Pitch.

The men on the jam saw her coming with breathless eagerness. Supper, fire, and bed were drawing just so much nearer to them every time that the ringing, iron-shod poles telegraphed above the rush of the waters a foot, a yard, a rod of distance lessened. The silent man rose and knocked the ashes out of his pipe. He put his hands to his lips. "Take the left of the big rock; don't try her inside!" He had been studying to some purpose, and now he came to the fore and helped to direct the boat, as dropping her cautiously, feeling their way inch by inch, partly by the light of the blazing torch, glaring red on the misty night, but more by that marvelous knowledge of the river which with the Fowlers was almost an instinct, Fowler and Spencer picked their way in the darkness among the rocks in the rising flood on that wild river.

The men on the jam hardly dared to look, for fear that even John Fowler might not be able to get down safe, and when they saw the boat go below them striving to make her turn and come up in the eddy, and the torch-light dim because it was burning down, they did not breathe for expectation that just as Spaulding's pole had snapped, so Spencer's would break on the same spot and leave them in despair. Then Fowler knocked the shaggy cinder from the top of the torch with his pole; the light blazed bright again; the boat loomed nearer; the flame leaped, and John Fowler swung her side against the jam.

Small time they lost in clambering in, four chilled and weary men of excellent cheerfulness. Then Spencer took the bow and gave the stern to John Fowler, that he might have the place requiring greatest skill, and they poled her back in safety to the eddy below Rhine's Pitch.

Four very wet and weary men tumbled ashore, and a Spencer more done-out than any of them. It is hard work to be a hero; he did not think of anything but going to

bed. Some brief but not fulsome thanks
were passed, no doubt, some credit for great
water-craft was bestowed, and then John
Fowler drove his oxen home, the children
walking beside him with their lantern.

At the river-drivers' camp the rescued
men were thinking of supper. The boy
was used up; he had crawled into the
spreads and lay shaking in an ague there,
because, even covered up head and ears, he
could not help seeing things. The silent
man took an axe, and the chip-chop of it
off one side showed that he was cutting
firewood. Tom Smith was getting pota-
toes out of a bag. The ex-soldier, bent
over a little pile of birch-bark and whit-
tlings, was starting a fire. No doubt he
was thinking of Moores and Spaulding,
for as he worked he sang softly, —

> " ' We 're tenting to-night on the old camp-ground,
> Give us a song to cheer.' "

Tom Smith, who, when he first landed,
had given three great sighs of relief and
then had begun to swear, — softly, very
deliberately, entirely without animus, like
the gentlest summer rain falling upon a

roof, just repeating over and over everything which he could remember, — had
turned his whole attention to supper.

" Boys," he said, " I 've just earned fair
a front seat in heaven for not swearing for
the three damnedest long hours that ever
was tooken out of a man's mortal life ; but
I 'd swap even off with any man who would
give me a roasted potato."

" ' Many are the hearts that are weary to-night,' "

chanted the old soldier, paying no attention to anything but his fire and his own
thoughts.

Just then, in the distance, far off, a
horned owl hooted.

A conscious smirk drew across Tom
Smith's face, and he clapped his hand
upon his mouth. " O hell, I forgot,"
he murmured like a child who has been
caught; " take it all back ag'in — ' Damn
a owl ' — that 's so ; but p'raps they might
give me a seat some'ers way back next the
door."

The old soldier did not hear him at all ;
he was keeping on with his song, and had
come to the refrain of it : —

" ' Tenting to-night,
Tenting to-night,
Tenting on the old camp-ground.' "

Lots of times before, too, the other fellow had been taken, and he had been
left.

No other man but one of the Fowlers
could have made that rescue; everybody
will tell you that. But who else could have
done what Spencer did? The water rose
that night and carried the jam away. A
little less persistence on his part, a little less
stubborn courage, a little more thought for
his own safety, a little more disregard for
other men's, and four men more would have
been added to the total of the casualties of
the river. That Spencer man came very
near being a hero. Only he was not the
fresh, sleek, well-groomed young fellow of
books, who never gets wet, or tired, or torn;
but just a rough, ragged, dirty, wrinkle-
faced, sun-burned, utterly dragged-out
man, with lame arms and sore fingers and
bruises from rough treatment, the sort of
man you pass on the street-corners, spring

and fall, and speak of as belonging to the "lower class."

Pray, who knows where St. Peter is going to put you and me and the Spencers when he calls us up by classes and ranks us by the work done in this world? Will only reading and writing and arithmetic count? or will he demand some proof of pluck, persistence, and generous action? It is likely enough that St. Peter knows by name even all of the Spencers, and for such a deed as this may award his highest honors, something not bestowed upon the nameless ones who make up the "cultured masses."

X

"JOYFULLY"

"JOYFULLY"

DRIVING logs on Sunday has always been accounted as a work of necessity : so many logs to be taken down on so much head of water, — it is almost a mathematical problem; and if the logs get "hung up," they are spoiled before another year, therefore it is a moral problem also whether it is better to break the Sabbath one's self or to break the owners of the logs financially. On Penobscot the custom is so firmly intrenched that perhaps no argument could avail to change it. Yet upon no point are the heads and the hands of the drive more divided. Some of the men have conscientious scruples about working Sundays; others know that it has been successfully discontinued elsewhere, and cite the example of the Androscoggin Drive, which more than twenty years ago discontinued driving on Sundays ; while all are agreed that in seven successive days of labor they cannot accomplish as much work as they could do in six days, if they had Sunday to rest in.

Still, there has never been any open strife upon the subject; the drive pays them seven days' wages when it knows that it is getting but six days' results; the men, realizing that it is not greed oppressing them but the demands of a military necessity, which must snatch the day for fear of the morrow's uncertainties, do their work, take their pay, and grumble privately. They feel that there is room for honest difference of opinion upon the subject, but it is not their campaign. That is the situation upon Penobscot.

This brief story relates how elsewhere a Penobscot man, keen to seize his opportunity, changed this established custom. It is a little comedy of conscience. With masterly adroitness Sebattis presses his point home to the other man's conscience, while he dexterously guards his own line of retreat in case he fails. It was no mere lucky fluke. Sebattis was a strategist to whom fine combinations were dear, as any one must acknowledge who ever sat down with him to a game of draughts, as any one might guess who noted his resemblance to the pictures of the Marquis Ito. To those who judge by externals only, perhaps he was nothing but a huge, fat, greasy Indian ; but in this little tale he reveals himself as a man of heart and judgment, jovial, shrewd, diplomatic, and disinterested, even long years before philanthropy became a fashion.

Dead is Sebattis, and his stories are forgotten. Few could tell you now how he made and recited them, long compositions, requiring sometimes two or three evenings for their full unfolding, yet carefully constructed with an eye to their effects, modeled as only an artist can mould a tale, and told without omissions or alterations because he had a respect for his own artistic creations. They were indeed works of art, and no one who ever hurt his artist's sensitiveness by falling asleep in the middle of an interminable tale will forget his plaintive reproach : "What for you gone 'sleep ? Why you don' gone 'wake ? " Then he would begin some

miles back in his story, wherever his lis-
tener had lost him, and tell it all over
again from that point, because he would
not mutilate a work of art.

Of all the countless stories that he
knew, perhaps the following is the only
one which can be reproduced at all as he
used to rehearse it, and even this is a con-
densed story. It would have taken Sebattis
a whole evening to tell this little story;
but even now, shorn of all its divagations, it
is still recognizably Big Sebattis Mitchell.

When supper was done and the camp-
fire burned briskly and the blankets were
laid out for lounging before the blaze, —
how it drew the resinous aroma from the
balsam boughs! — then Big Sebattis
would begin to untangle the threads of the
stories in his memory. " Never we told
you it that story 'bout Old Isaac sung um
' Joyfully ' ? " would be his introduction.
Then with slow speech and many pauses
he would begin the tale.

" Well, we shall told you all 'bout it.
You see that time she live it Old Isaac
Maccadavy " — that is, at Magaguadavic.

" Good many years ben lumber there Old Isaac. We ben live there ourself eight years, work it Old Isaac, kind under-boss, you see.

"One night in fall come Old Isaac my house, spoke so, ' Sebattis, we wan' you gone up ribber to-mollow mornin' berry arly.'

" You see on Maccadavy he don't drove it all logs clear down in sprin' like here; always he lef' part dribe at foot lower lake; then when he want logs in fall, he have um fall dribe.

" Well, nex' mornin' we gone with um Old Isaac in waggin. When we come where high bridge cross ribber, speak so Old Isaac, ' We wan' you stay dis place pick it off logs so he don' jam on 'butments.'

" You see dis bridge he have 'butments, he don' have middle pier. Log he catch on 'butment, s'pose don't pick um off he wing out an' make jam. He give me axe an' peavey, an' coil of riggin', speak so, ' You got it good board dat house; you stay here till we come back.'

" Soon 's he gone Old Isaac, we took it

two long logs; we snipe it one end " —
illustrating by the pantomime of sharp-
ening his finger-tip — " then we rung it
odder end, so " — that is, cut a ring around
it. " Then we tied it one end each side
stream to stump 'bove bridge and let it
laid out slantin' 'gainst 'butment like shear-
boom. Then when log struck, she sheer
off and gone through bridge hisself.

" Well, we stuck um up peavey in log.
We smoke; we whittle — hab berry good
time; we board house, had not'in' do.
Sometimes we wet it peavey so he don't
slip off lings " — that is, rings.

" When we ben there 'bout two weeks,
Sat'day night come long Old Isaac. Spoke
so, ' Sebahttis, you hab hard work ? '

" We tell um, ' Yes, we hab ber' hard
wo'k ; hab wet it dat peavey good many
times keep it on lings.'

" Speak so Isaac, ' You wan' gone down
home ? '

" We tell um, ' Sartin.'

" Well, say so then, ' You got it in
waggin.'

" Well, we got it in waggin. We start

down ribber — ribber an' road he run
same way. Took out pipe Old Isaac; then
she took it out tobacker, an' fill it his pipe;
then she stuck it up his feet on fender;
then she begun smoke an' sung um 'Joyfully.'"

Sebattis never said anything more about
this song, but it probably was: —

> "Joyfully, joyfully, onward we move,
>   Bound to the land of bright spirits above."

"We speak so, 'What for make it you
sing um "Joyfully," Isaac?'

"Says so, 'Don't you heard about it?
I'm Chreestyun man.'

"'Ah-h-h-h! How long first?'"

One knowing Sebattis can well understand that his simple interrogation was as
full of meaning as Lord Burleigh's nod.
It was a caustic comment on all his employer's past, and a pleasantly satiric doubt
whether the future was to be any different.
We observe how Old Isaac changes the
subject; how Sebattis refuses to allow him
to escape and still follows with his irony,
a grave and delicate mockery in disavowal
of his being taken in by such chaff.

" Then he say, ' Why you no smoke, S'bahtees ? '

" We say, ' We Chreestyun man, *we* don't smoke; 'sides, he charge it dollar and half pound out wangan for tobacker,[1] we cahn' 'ford it.'

" Then she took it out big piece to-backer; she cut it in two, give me half; speak so, ' Nebber you want it tobacker long 's you work me.'

" We say so, ' To-mollow mornin' Sunday, Isaac.'

" ' Yes ! '

" ' You goin' dribin' to-mollow ? '

" ' Sartin ! '

" ' Ugh-h-h-*huh !* ' " Sebattis could put a great deal of expression into a grunt.

" ' Why you ask we goin' dribin' to-mollow ? '

" ' Only we want know.' " Sebattis knew when to be indifferent.

" ' You t'ink he ain't right dribin' Sunday ? '

---

[1] " Wangan " (pronounced wong-un) here means the supplies furnished by Isaac and sold to his men at exorbitant profits. In most places it is about equivalent to " outfit," and includes the commissary and cooking equipment.

"'Sartin ! Right *me* dribe um Sunday ;
we don't sing it " Joyfully."'

"Then she keep smoke, smoke Old
Isaac. Then bime-by she speak so : 'You
t'ink ain't right dribin' Sunday ?'

"'Sartin ; right *me* dribin' Sunday ;
we don' sung um " Joyfully." S'pose we
Chreestyun man, we sung it " Joyfully,"
we don' dribin' Sunday.'

"Then great while she smoke Ol' Isaac.
Bime-by she spoke so, 'S'bahtees, you
ride horse ?'

"We speak so, ' Sartin !'

"'To-mollow mornin' he 's Sunday.'

"We speak so, 'Yes !'

"'Now to-mollow mornin', S'bahtees,
berry arly we want you took it dis horse
an' gone up ribber. S'pose you found any
crews on logs, you tell um stop. When
you got up dam, s'pose he ben h'ist, you
tell um " Shut down ;" s'pose he don't
ben h'ist, you tell um not h'ist.'

"Next mornin' berry arly, we took it
horse, we gone up ribber, — ribber an'
road he run same way, road close 'longside
of ribber. Fog on ribber so you can' see.

"Bime-by we hear it peavey sclatch on laidge; we know crew was pickin' on middle-jam. We lef' it horse, we gone down ribber, says, ' Hullo, boys !'

"Speaks so, ' What you want ? '

"We say, ' Come 'shore !'

"He want know what for.

"We tell um, ' Dem 's orders, headquarters. Old Isaac she's Chreestyun man, sung it " Joyfully,"—no more dribin' Sunday.'

"Eb'ry crew we come to we tolt it dat same way. When we got dam she ben h'ist 'bout twenty minits.

"We speak so, ' You shut down, boys ; dem 's orders, headquarters ; Old Isaac she sung it " Joyfully ; " no more dribin' Sunday.'

"Speaks so, ' We wish you brought it us dat same word eb'ry Sunday.'

"Two more years we work it Old Isaac, no more dribin' Sunday."